"Could You Put Lipstick On M... Or A Woman's Phone Number In My Pocket?"

"Is that the way it would be?" Bel asked.

"I don't know." Jake paused. "It's likely, given my past."

"So—you just want me to live with you, no promises? No marriage, no children?"

He winced at this painting of the picture, but she was right.

"You said compromise, Jake. But it seems to me that what you mean is, *I* compromise."

He lifted his head, his eyes dark and tormented. "I'll marry you if that's what you say you want!"

Bel sat gazing into his eyes. She seemed to see straight into his soul, to the man who would make the right husband for her. She saw honesty, decency, a determination to do right, intelligence, passion, deep love…and a man who had been taught to doubt himself for being a man.

She felt her whole life was waiting with bated breath for her decision.…

Dear Reader,

Welcome in the millennium, and the 20th anniversary of Silhouette, with Silhouette Desire—where you're guaranteed powerful, passionate and provocative love stories that feature rugged heroes and spirited heroines who experience the full emotional intensity of falling in love!

We are happy to announce that the ever-fabulous Annette Broadrick will give us the first MAN OF THE MONTH of the 21st century, *Tall, Dark & Texan.* A highly successful Texas tycoon opens his heart and home to a young woman who's holding a secret. Lindsay McKenna makes a dazzling return to Desire with *The Untamed Hunter,* part of her highly successful MORGAN'S MERCENARIES: THE HUNTERS miniseries. Watch sparks fly when a hard-bitten mercenary is reunited with a spirited doctor—the one woman who got away.

A Texan Comes Courting features another of THE KEEPERS OF TEXAS from Lass Small's miniseries. A cowboy discovers the woman of his dreams—and a shocking revelation. Alexandra Sellers proves a virginal heroine can bring a Casanova to his knees in *Occupation: Casanova.* Desire's themed series THE BRIDAL BID debuts with Amy J. Fetzer's *Going...Going...Wed!* And in *Conveniently His,* Shirley Rogers presents best friends turned lovers in a marriage-of-convenience story.

Each and every month, Silhouette Desire offers you six exhilarating journeys into the seductive world of romance. So start off the new millennium right, by making a commitment to sensual love and treating yourself to all six!

Enjoy!

Joan Marlow Golan
Senior Editor, Silhouette Desire

Please address questions and book requests to:
Silhouette Reader Service
U.S.: 3010 Walden Ave., P.O. Box 1325, Buffalo, NY 14269
Canadian: P.O. Box 609, Fort Erie, Ont. L2A 5X3

Occupation: Casanova

ALEXANDRA SELLERS

Silhouette® Desire®

Published by Silhouette Books
America's Publisher of Contemporary Romance

SILHOUETTE BOOKS

ISBN 0-373-76264-X

OCCUPATION: CASANOVA

Copyright © 1999 by Alexandra Sellers

All rights reserved. Except for use in any review, the reproduction or utilization of this work in whole or in part in any form by any electronic, mechanical or other means, now known or hereafter invented, including xerography, photocopying and recording, or in any information storage or retrieval system, is forbidden without the written permission of the editorial office, Silhouette Books, 300 East 42nd Street, New York, NY 10017 U.S.A.

All characters in this book have no existence outside the imagination of the author and have no relation whatsoever to anyone bearing the same name or names. They are not even distantly inspired by any individual known or unknown to the author, and all incidents are pure invention.

This edition published by arrangement with Harlequin Books S.A.

® and TM are trademarks of Harlequin Books S.A., used under license. Trademarks indicated with ® are registered in the United States Patent and Trademark Office, the Canadian Trade Marks Office and in other countries.

Visit us at www.romance.net

Printed in U.S.A.

ALEXANDRA SELLERS

Canadian-born and raised, Alexandra Sellers first came to London as a drama student. She lives near Hampstead Heath with her husband, Nick. They share housekeeping with Monsieur, a beautiful tabby, who came in through the window one day and announced that he was staying.

Alexandra loves the people, languages, religions and history of Central Asia and the Middle East. She has studied Hebrew and Farsi (Persian) and is currently working on Arabic. She is the author of over twenty-five novels and a cat language textbook.

What she would miss most on a desert island is shared laughter.

Readers can write to Alexandra at P.O. Box 9449, London NW3 2WH, UK.

To my brother Gord
Everything a brother should be

One

―

"**Y**ou may kiss your bride."

The bride had never looked lovelier as she tilted a tremulous face up to her new husband's lips, and that, Bel reflected, was saying something. Her sister Tallia was breathtakingly beautiful under the worst conditions. Today she was beyond description.

Over Brad's shoulder, she couldn't help noticing the hunger with which Jake, Brad's best man, had his eyes glued to the couple. Not for the first time she wondered just how deep the groom's best friend's feelings for the bride went.

It was about a year since she had first heard Jake's name, ten months since she had her first and only date with her sister's fiancé's best friend.

Over dinner, he had confided to Bel how desperately he had tried to "save" his lifelong best friend, Brad, from the fate worse than death that he knew was beckoning—

marriage. He spoke very amusingly, but Bel sensed a real truth under the smiling demeanour. He had not wanted his friend to get serious with her sister. Even then, Bel had been dubious about the real motives under Jake's determination to keep Brad away from Tallia. Now she wondered if he still thought his friend was making a mistake, whether he still wished he had been able to prevent this happening.

Brad was prolonging the kiss, and the congregation began to stir with amusement. Bel's eyes lingered on Jake Drummond.

He was dark like his friend, and very attractive, but he had a more saturnine cast to his features. He looked like a devil, a rogue, his eyebrows slanting over his dark eyes, his mouth for once a little grim, not tilting with the usual smile of dry amusement.

Bel knew his looks didn't lie. He *was* a rogue, in the old-fashioned sense of the word. He was cynical about women and love and marriage and faithfulness and probably nearly everything else she herself held dear. She had found out that much over that dinner.

She had found out more than that. She had found out how devastatingly attractive a rogue could be, how easily and deeply he could burrow under her skin—and stay there—in spite of all her intentions to the contrary. She had found out just how fragile her determination would be, if it were ever seriously challenged by Jake Drummond.

She had learned she had better stay away from temptation, if she wanted to keep the vow she'd made at seventeen. For the four years since then it hadn't been too difficult to keep—even though all the friends who had so solemnly sworn with her were succumbing, one by one. But she'd looked at Jake that night and felt something very, very different from anything she'd felt before from a man—and she'd suddenly had a very clear idea of what the phrase "putty in his hands" would mean.

It would mean waking up and realizing that you'd given away your virginity to someone who would make a mark on his gun butt, smile, salute, and then move on.

Leaving you with nothing but a memory. And a seedy memory at that.

Be careful around woman chasers, Bel, they won't care how they get you or how much it costs you, and they'll leave you feeling used, her mother had advised her, and she knew it was good advice.

Bel sighed and looked away as Brad at last lifted his lips from his bride's willing mouth and, with one strong, possessive arm behind her back, turned with her to face the smiling congregation.

Jake Drummond blinked and came out of his trance. He wasn't sure how long he'd been staring at Brad and Tallia, trying to figure out what the hell was happening to him. He'd watched his friend take his new bride in his arms, and although he'd seen Brad with a fair quota of women, he knew he'd never seen him like this before—deeply and possessively and maybe even selflessly in love. Repeating his vows with a voice that said he'd never meant anything more.

But it wasn't supposed to affect Jake like this, make him wonder what was missing in his own life or if he'd ever feel that way about a woman. He knew he wouldn't. He had the word *philanderer* imprinted in his genes, as his grandmother had been so fond of telling him. He didn't have it in him to get permanently attached to one woman—if any man did. And he was too honest ever to try to fool himself or any woman. He was always upfront. He always said from the beginning he wasn't there for the long run.

He was a Casanova. It was in his blood.

His eyes refocused just beyond the newlyweds and settled on Tallia's dark-haired sister. Bel was looking as gorgeous as her fabulous sister in her bridesmaid's dress, and anyway he'd never had much of a thing for blondes. He'd seen her a few times since the fall, but only at Brad's place, when they had both been invited to dinner. And she had never once accepted his offer to drive her home.

There had been women over the years who had opted out of a fling with Jake once he had explained about himself. What irked him about Bel was that he hadn't had time to get around to explaining about himself. Bel had opted out before she even knew about his track record, which argued that she just didn't like him.

For his own part, he had felt a strong attraction to Tallia's little sister. It had been a bit of a shock to realize that for once his charm left a woman cold.

Well, hell, you win some, you lose some. Jake tried to shrug but found he was frowning moodily instead. It was true, he'd have preferred to win Annabel Venables. Women didn't normally get under his skin, but she'd done that somehow, right that first night over dinner. Looking at him with those wide, serious hazel eyes that seemed to make most of his jokes go flat.

Not that she didn't have a sense of humour. He'd seen her face light up with appreciation whenever something really amusing was in the air, and her quick laughter was one of the things he found attractive about her. But she didn't seem to have developed a taste for the kind of ego-stroking sexual wordplay that usually made women smile at him speculatively.

And then come to bed with him.

And without it, he'd been at a loss for how to get her into bed.

Win some, lose some.

She was looking very good at the moment, though—her wide eyes more green than brown in the silky green off-the-shoulder dress with a skirt made of floating panels, that made her look as if she were coming out of the sea; her neck, encircled by a tiny strand of gold braid like golden seaweed, looking so sexually vulnerable his loins ached; her mouth, usually set in firm, common-sense lines, softened into a trembling smile today. Her skin, lightly tanned though it was only June, glowed with health and vitality. Her thick brown hair was caught up in a wreath of flowers that matched Tallia's huge bouquet and her own, both of which she was now holding, the clusters of white blooms giving her an air of sweet innocence that pulled at his jaded heart in a way that sweet innocence never had before.

He'd never had a taste for innocence; he liked his women experienced. That way there was less chance of breaking hearts. But of course with looks like hers Bel wasn't a virgin. Not at age—what was she? Twenty-two, Tallia had said. He could believe a lot about small-town men, but that they were as slow as that he did not believe. Besides, she'd been at university in Vancouver, and Jake remembered with deep fondness his own wild university days. Still, he knew men who liked the look even though there was nothing behind it.

Not him.

The worst thing a man like you can do to a woman is destroy her innocence, Jake, his grandmother had always told him. *I hope you'll never do that.*

Bel was smiling mistily as she looked at Brad and Tallia, and Jake wondered if she was maybe a little more taken with her sister's husband than she should be.

For the first time he wondered if that might explain why, after only one meal together, any time he had called and tried to date her, she had turned him down. Not dislike of him, maybe, but reluctance to get involved with Brad's best friend? It would explain a lot—like why he had been so sure they had discovered a mutual attraction at that dinner but she cold-decked him every time afterwards.

Tallia turned to receive her bouquet back from her sister. As bride and groom started down the aisle and Jake and Bel moved closer together, Bel's gaze shifted and caught his. Just for a moment he thought he saw alarm in her eyes, but then she smiled, and he figured he was mistaken. It was a cool smile, nothing more in it than a nod to her brother-in-law's friend.

As they followed the newlyweds down the aisle he didn't resist the impulse to put a guiding arm around her waist. He hardly ever did resist the impulse to touch her, but he saw her so rarely that didn't mean much. She had a way of slipping away from him, but today, he figured, she couldn't do that. This was one of those traditional weddings, where the bride had been given to the husband by her father and—as the minister had explained at the rehearsal—when the ceremony was over, the groom swept the bride completely around, keeping her in his left arm, by tradition leaving his sword arm free to defend her against all comers.

That good old stuff.

So by inference the bridesmaid was a frail woman in need of his powerful masculine supporting arm, however capable she was every other day of her life.

He smiled down at her as his hand rested against her waist. Bel flicked a green, unreadable look up at him, and then firmly turned her face away.

"Oooh, my!" In the pew beside him a middle-aged woman in a dark blue straw hat whispered happily to her neighbour, as though she had just discovered a thrilling possibility *there*.

The devil in him urged him to say, *Forget it, madam. I am not the marrying kind, and even if I were she wouldn't have me,* but he resisted. Instead he concentrated on the attractive contradiction of cool warmth coming from Bel's skin through the soft cloth of her dress.

Electric heat from Jake Drummond's hand burned into her. After the first shock, as if he had planted a jungle vine in her flesh, Bel could feel tendrils of vibrant warmth grow up through her body, enclosing her arm, her back, her breast in its pliant caress. She felt it wrap her nipple.

The tingle of responsive yearning stirred into life, her body wanting to lean into his, to wrap him in return. She could not prevent the first instinctive melting, but she was quick to take control. Bel bit her lip and took a deep breath, straightening her back infinitesimally. *He's playing songs of sex, but not for you,* she reminded herself firmly. She was careful not to look his way again.

But she was aware of his touch all the way. She wondered if maybe he was doing it deliberately, knowing what it was doing to her, as a kind of joke. Jake was experienced, that was for sure, so it wasn't beyond the bounds of possibility that he had sussed out that she was physically attracted but resisting it. She supposed a guy who was a rogue might play a game like that to amuse himself.

Outside the little church, which looked very human-built and fragile against the circle of rough mountains in the warm afternoon sunshine, people were laughing and calling and hugging and kissing and taking pictures and throwing rice. The official photographer was waving them over to the pre-chosen picturesque backdrop, and Bel quite naturally slipped out of Jake's hold and went over to put her arms around her sister.

"It was lovely," she whispered. "It just went beautifully!"

All around them people were saying the same thing. What a beautiful service, what nice hymns, what a lovely atmosphere, and didn't the church look marvellous with all the flowers and with the sun glowing through the stained glass!

Jake shook Brad's hand without saying very much. He wasn't sure he knew how to talk to his best buddy anymore. He wondered where their friendship would go from here, because anyone who thought marriage didn't change a man was a fool.

Brad already looked different, which was pretty weird considering he and Tallia had been living together since Christmas and had already bought, if not moved into, their new house. They'd been *acting* married for months, so how come Brad had that newlywed glow on him now? It was a mystery, and one Jake didn't figure he'd ever fathom.

Your grandfather was a man who should never have married, and neither should you.

"Congratulations, Brad," he said. "Knew you could do it."

Before Brad could respond, the photographer's assistant was there, pushing and directing them into position.

"Now, will you all please be careful to ignore all the other cameras and look at Yorgo, because he's the official photographer and we want everybody's eye line the same," she instructed them firmly.

She was young and sure of herself, if not much more than five-four. Jake sent a smiling glance of appreciation down at her. "You seemed a lot taller when I was in fourth grade," he observed.

She laughed and flicked a glance at him, and it was pretty clear that she liked what she saw. "For that, you stay behind after class,'' she ordered with a nod, and then strode over to clear a chattering group from the sight lines.

It was the sort of invitation he might once have followed up on, but although she had the kind of edge he'd always liked, the quality that said she could look after herself and wasn't going to leave herself open to hurt, he knew he wouldn't.

This was happening far too often lately. In fact, Jake realized with a little shock, it was happening all the time. He watched the woman with narrowed eyes, wondering just when it was that the fun had gone out of the game for him.

He tried to think back. In the fall, he'd had to fly to Hong Kong for one of his clients. Hong Kong was a great city and he usually enjoyed it, but he remembered feeling under too much pressure of work to take up his client's generous offers to show him the nightlife. Was that the beginning?

Hell! Could it be that long ago? A little desperately, Jake tried to remember the sequence of events. He came home from Hong Kong with a flu bug…he could remember a few telephone calls from women irritated by his lack of interest and their frank disbelief that he was too ill to see anyone.

But it was true, he just didn't have any interest in the kind of nights his women friends were used to—food, drink, music and sex, not necessarily in that order. He figured he must have been overworked before he even went to Hong Kong, and the bug really got to him.…

''Everybody looking this way, please! Big smile, all!''

He had called Bel once, maybe because he thought she'd be happy with a quieter evening, just talking over dinner the way they'd done that night, and then a walk on the sea wall with the ocean stirring in the night, but she'd said she was busy.

"Again, please, smile…thank you!"

Actually, he'd called her a couple of times, thinking maybe she was irritated because he had left it so long. He'd explained that he'd been in Hong Kong, but she was still busy.

"Both immediate families, please…is that everyone? Thank you, and smile…thank you.

"Could we have all members of both families with the wedding party now, please? My goodness, are there really so many of you?"

Absently, Jake moved where he was pushed, stood where he was told.

He guessed he'd phoned a few times after that, too, he didn't quite remember how often. Finally she'd told him she was studying hard for her final year's exams and just wasn't free to date at all. So he quit calling and put her out of his mind. That must have been in early spring.

He remembered now—it had been February 7. He'd wanted to take her out for Valentine's Day, which was pretty stupid, because most women would take that as a sign of something. But fortunately she'd said she was busy till May…

"A little closer, please, look this way…that's it…and smile.…"

Tallia was living in Brad's apartment by then, and whenever Jake visited, which was pretty often, he'd caught himself thinking that men like Brad, who had the gene for settling down, were luckier than men like himself, in the long run. He'd never believed that before—but then, who at the age of twenty-five ever thinks things are going to change? Who ever imagines they'll feel differently at the age of thirty-three?

"Now, could we have just the wedding party, please, bride, groom, bridesmaid, best man, but everyone else, please don't disappear…"

But Jake told himself he hadn't actually changed. He'd figured it was just that flu bug still making him tired. He would get over it and be his old self any day.

And now here it was June! He'd been living practically like a *monk* for two, three…more than *seven months!*

It was the worst case of Hong Kong flu he'd ever heard of.

"A little closer in to the groom, please, best man."

Jake obeyed the photographer's assistant moodily, knowing she was interested and that if he caught her eye she would smile a promise at him, knowing he did not want to catch her eye. Unconsciously, he turned his head, looked past Brad and Tallia and found his eyes resting on Bel.

"Look this way, please!"

She looked radiant in the sun, not glowing with happiness like Tallia, but fresh, young, facing life with a confidence that was deeply attractive.

"This way, please, best man!"

Jake started and turned his head, only to catch the eye of the woman in the blue hat, who was smiling knowingly—who was, he realized irritably, *simpering* at him.

He turned towards the photographer. *It is not what you think, madam,* he informed the stupid woman silently. *I have no plans for settling down with the woman you imagine or any other. I am not the marrying kind.*

Two

Bel sank down onto the seat of the low sports car as Jake held the door.

"Should I put up the top?" he asked.

Bel shook her head. "I brought a scarf."

She had not protested when Tallia had proposed that she drive to the reception venue with the best man. This was her sister's day. She knew that Tallia was hoping, even after so long, that Bel and Jake might get together, and that a little enforced proximity might trigger something. She hadn't had the heart to tell Tallia what Jake had said about a fate worse than death, or his attempts to save Brad from it. And she certainly hadn't confessed that she found Jake dangerously attractive and a threat to her, so Tallia could hardly be blamed for this traditional arrangement.

But she wished pretty fervently that some other arrangement had been made. And as she had no intention of *leaving* the reception with the best man, she had taken the trouble to ask her brother Russ to drive up here with her so she could get Tallia's car to the hotel parking lot before the wedding.

As she slipped her well-shaped legs inside the seat well, the long flower tendrils of her bridesmaid's bouquet trailed out of her lap and down over the doorjamb almost to the pavement. Jake bent and lifted them out of harm's way. As he stood with his hand carefully cupping the quivering blossoms their eyes met.

The gesture whispered through her with its own particular storm. She would be in his hands just like that, if she allowed it to happen. His dark fingers looked strong and very masculine as they cradled the tender flowers, and his eyes were filled with promise, and for one moment of piercing sweetness she longed to deliver the burden of her virginity into such capable care.

Then Jake set the flowers down against her thighs, straightened, and closed the door. Bel sat shivering under the impact of the moment, her eyes suddenly blind. When her vision cleared again, Jake was in the seat beside her and she was gazing down at the tumbled blooms in her green-clad lap.

He started the engine, then turned to her. "Want to put on that scarf now?"

He was so tuned to a woman's needs! She supposed that was how a man like him managed to get to so many women—with a caring that couldn't possibly go very deep. She'd be smart to keep her guard up. It would be fatal to take it personally or let herself be affected by it.

With a wordless nod she opened her little green handbag and pulled out the scarf. When she had secured it around her hair and its wreath of flowers, Jake let out the clutch and with a low grumbly purr the car moved out of the church parking lot and onto the narrow country road after the white limousine carrying the bridal couple.

One fragile white petal had come adrift and lay against her knee. Absently, she picked it up and held it between finger and thumb, letting the wind carry it away.

Maybe she should have done that with her virginity ages ago—just let it be carried off in the prevailing wind. Then it wouldn't be such a deep and catastrophic question whether to give in to what she felt for Jake now. She could sleep with him without worrying about the aftermath. It wouldn't be that big a deal.

"Wondering whether to cast your pearls before swine?"

She gasped as he spoke, then struggled to cover her reaction and flicked her eyes up to his profile. He was watching the road.

"I didn't know I had that option."

"Sure you did," he contradicted her levelly. He changed down for an approaching hill and looked at her with a blackness that swallowed the sun. "Why won't you date me, Annabel?"

"I think that's my business, isn't it?"

"Why won't you date me?"

She could sense something like angry contempt in his tone, and that responsively angered her.

"I'm not interested in dating you."

"Why not?"

She turned to him, exasperated. "What do you want, a list of your failings?"

"Yes."

She shook her head, torn between frustration and the powerful need to touch him. She could never remember feeling such a physical pull in her life, as primary as gravity. She wished now that she *had* confided in Tallia, and pleaded to avoid this little ride. But Tallia was so hopeful, and of course she believed in the power of love, and she would have argued that Jake might change...and anyway, Bel herself really hadn't believed that a short drive in his company would undermine her determination.

But sexual magnetism apparently had a very strong pull.

She tried to resist his force of personality, but it was either speak or act. It was impossible to resist all reaction to him.

"I think you know your failings. You don't need me to outline them," she said at last, feeling like a weakling. As if she had lost points, if anyone were keeping score.

Jake might be, of course.

"Outline them for me. The ones that bother you."

His voice was seductive to her senses even when he didn't seem to mean it to be. The low-voiced tone of command, cutting through the noise of the wind, almost melted her.

"Jake, what is it exactly that you want?" she demanded.

He glanced over; it was impossible to take his eyes off the winding mountain road for more than a second.

"I want to see you." *See* being a euphemism, of course, Bel told herself ruthlessly. "You don't want to see me. So I would like you to tell me why."

Anger lowered her guard; she cracked.

"I suppose because I get the feeling that to you *see* and *sex* are interchangeable words."

He changed gear again. His arm moved with such muscled fluidity—or was that just her own suppressed sexuality talking? She felt a constant electric awareness of Jake's physical being, like a thousand acupuncture needles all down her side, from scalp to ankle.

"And they're not to you."

"To me the x is a significant letter change," she agreed firmly.

He nodded several times, then negotiated a couple of hairpin curves with flawless timing. They had climbed out of the valley and the vista suddenly opened. The church lay nestled below them among its encircling trees, while all around it fields of neat farms and apple orchards stretched along the valley floor. Between the trees, on a curve above them, she caught glimpses of the white bridal limousine.

"Do you have a lot of experience of sex, Bel?" he asked in that same level tone.

So he hadn't guessed. She wondered if it would shock him if she told him the truth. "Not a lot."

"I didn't think so. If you had, you'd realize that the words *see* and *sex* are interchangeable between you and me, not because of any predisposition on my part, but because one of us is kerosene and the other is a bonfire."

His words, delivered in a low, intense tone, sent a shock of violent anticipation through her. Bel had to close her eyes for a moment. Did he really believe that? Did he feel that strongly about her? Or was he— Yes, of course he had to talk like that to any woman he had targeted, she reminded herself—convince each one she was sexually special.

The thought meant she could control her voice. "I'm sure that in your very active life you've met lots of cans of kerosene, Jake."

Something in him wanted to say that it had never been quite like this. But he knew that would sound like a promise, and he wouldn't make any promise he knew he'd never keep. He had never led a woman on with pledges for the future, never once lied to get someone into bed.

He'd never really needed to. There weren't that many women who asked for a guarantee of undying devotion. Mostly what they wanted—implicitly or explicitly—was the guarantee of sexual expertise and a good time, and he had no qualms about giving that.

"And I guess you've met your share of bonfires. But— how old are you—twenty-two?"

His level intensity was making her more and more nervous. Until now she'd had no idea that Jake had particularly targeted her. She had believed that his calls were simply the result of his regularly going through his list of phone numbers. And more than once it had crossed her mind that he knew she was resisting a powerful attraction and was merely baiting her.

If someone as experienced, as attractive as Jake really set out to get her—how would she ever be able to resist?

"Forgive me if I don't instantly respond to your probing questions about my private life."

Maybe he should have guessed that Bel would be different. She struck him as a very brainy, very modern girl, and he'd heard that brainy modern girls were taking a good look at the facts these days and thinking hard about what they did. He hadn't messed with anyone as young as she was practically since he was that age himself.

He wondered if it would make a difference if he assured her he hadn't had unprotected sex for something like thirteen years. He glanced at her. Probably not.

"Do you mind my knowing your age?"

"I mind being told I am not old enough to understand the choices I'm making."

He grimaced ruefully.

"What are you looking for, Bel, a promise of forever? Forever's rare these days."

He wondered how the hell he had gotten into this conversation. He hadn't planned to challenge her.

"I am looking for someone who is at least willing to consider that forever might exist," she said. She was calm and sure of herself, not swayed by his faint mockery. He liked that. "And I think that lets you out, doesn't it?"

Don't you ever lie to a good woman about your intentions. The other kind won't ask, so you don't have to worry there.

Of course his grandmother's ideas were hopelessly out of date—even when he was only a kid he had known that, but he had never made the mistake of trying to explain that to her.

He realized with distant astonishment that he was doing something he had never stooped to in all his life before— trying to argue an unwilling woman into bed. It was a cardinal rule of his not to push himself on a woman who wasn't interested. But he didn't seem to be able to stop.

"I am not the marrying kind, Bel, if that's what you're asking. Nevertheless, we could experience something rare together."

"If only you had a dollar for every time you've said that to a woman, eh?"

"I have never said that to any woman but you."

Bel bit her lip as her heart suddenly discovered overdrive. It was entirely new to her, but she didn't want to believe this kind of attraction was also rare for Jake. Because that probably meant that statistically, her chances of running into a feeling like this again soon were small. If she didn't meet someone to whom she was so powerfully attracted again, would she remain a virgin? Or would she end up in bed with someone no different than any other guy? And in that case, wouldn't it be better to give in to this now, even though there was no future in it?

She swiftly put a brake on that little insidious line of reasoning, and again found refuge in the belief that he was lying.

"I guess there are some things more important to me

than sexual pleasure,'' she said, knowing as she said it that she was a complete fraud. She had very little idea how important sexual pleasure might be to her. And when she was sitting close beside Jake it did seem as though it might be a lot more important than she had previously thought.

He turned his head and the black eyes consumed her again. ''You've had some pretty poor lovers,'' he observed, his voice filled with contempt for any man who could leave a woman like her talking like that about sex. He felt the mix of anger and satisfaction course through him—anger that anyone had treated her so clumsily, satisfaction that he would be the one to show her how good it could be.

She shrugged.

They had turned off on a wide drive, and a few yards away a pair of massive gates blocked the way. Jake pulled up behind the white limousine that carried Tallia and Brad, threw the gearshift into neutral, then turned, lifted a hand, and with a touch like cat's fur stroked her cheek.

It was totally unexpected, and Bel couldn't repress the shiver of pure, starving longing that rippled through her.

''There's a lot more to sex than you've been given,'' he said softly.

Oh, for sure. Bel closed her eyes, furious with herself, with him, with the whole stupid mess of sex, vows, promises, seduction and virginity. She took a deep breath and met his caressing smile with stony eyes.

''Suppose I said yes, Jake. And suppose we had a few wild nights. And suppose it really was rare and I never met that again. Do you really think I would prefer to go through the rest of my life regretting that sex would never be like that again, rather than simply never having experienced it at all?''

He had no answer. He had simply never looked at it from that perspective before.

"In your opinion, sexual pleasure is an end in itself," Bel went on, fervently, as if she had to convince herself, too. "In my opinion, the purpose of sexual pleasure is to bind two people in a loving relationship." She lifted her shoulders expressively. "Don't you think there are some positions so far apart compromise between them is simply not possible?"

A horn sounded. The gates were open and the limo had pulled away. A long line of cars now stretched out behind them as the wedding guests caught up with each other. A second driver, perhaps mistaking the motives of the first, also honked loudly, and suddenly the air was filled with a cacophony of happy horns. Jake let in the clutch and moved off after the limo along the winding drive.

They didn't speak again until he had pulled up in front of the hotel's impressive facade. A bellboy opened Bel's door and a uniformed valet driver opened Jake's, and in a minute they were standing on the pavement with Brad and Tallia as the other cars pulled up.

The bride and her bridesmaid immediately disappeared towards the Ladies, a luxuriously fitted and carpeted room filled with mirrors and plush chairs, the toilets themselves in an adjoining room.

Bel took off her scarf, then pulled a comb out of her purse and turned her attention to her sister. "Let's get you settled first," she said, and Tallia obediently sat down on a small velvet-cushioned bench in front of a dressing table.

"Did it really go all right, Bel?" she asked, as Bel tweaked her curls into order and straightened the flowers that held the veil in place. "I was so...I don't know, wrapped in some kind of cocoon with just Brad!"

Bel smiled tenderly. "That was pretty obvious. The ceremony was beautiful. There was a wonderful atmosphere and Brad just looked as though—well, as though he'd found the Holy Grail!''

Of course she wondered if one day a man would look at her like that. If no one ever did, would she regret what she had passed up with Jake?

"Stand up so I can straighten your dress."

As always, Bel's presence was having a calming effect on Tallia.

"Oh, thank you! You're always so cool, Bel, I wish I could be like you!''

Bel smiled and twitched the silky skirt of the white dress smooth. Funny how even Tal could think she was cool when her brain was buzzing with confusion and excitement.

When Tallia was ready, Bel turned her eyes to her own outfit. She was a pretty good foil for her sister in the slim emerald-green dress with its floaty panels, her smooth brown hair caught up with white and green flowers—Tallia white and blond with flecks of green, Bel green and brown with flecks of white.

"I'm sort of a poor man's version of you," she said when she had finished neatening her hair and the two beautiful girls stood side by side and looked at themselves in the mirror.

Tallia merely laughed and threw her sister an affectionate look. "I never heard before that Jake was poor, exactly.''

"Jake is interested in a fling. I'm not."

"Don't be so sure."

"Of which thesis?"

"Either." Tallia turned and turquoise eyes gazed into hazel ones. "You be sure to catch my bouquet, and see what happens."

"You don't understand Jake Drummond," Bel murmured.

"I understand how attractive you are, and how attracted he is to you," Tallia insisted. "We better go."

They were serving drinks and canapés in an elegant, extremely attractive lounge. When the two sisters entered, a member of staff quietly approached. "If you would care to give me your bouquets, I'll place them on the table for you," she said, so that was that little problem in logistics disposed of.

Brad and Jake were standing together in a group of laughing guests. Bel's eyes began combing the crowd for a group she would feel comfortable just walking up to and joining, but there were an awful lot of people here she didn't know. Then Tallia took the decision out of her hands, linking her arm through her sister's and leading her irresistibly along.

When they reached Brad's group, it parted for them, automatically creating a space beside Brad and another beside Jake. Jake smiled and handed Bel a flute glass.

"I saved you some champagne."

"Thank you," she said dubiously, accepting it.

Brad, meanwhile, with the merest raised eyebrow, had drawn two of the waiters hurrying over to offer their trays to Tallia.

"'Saved?'" Bel repeated with a raised eyebrow. There were at least fifty glasses within arm's reach.

Jake took a glass for himself. "There might have been a run on the bank. There are several very heavy drinkers in the room."

He lifted the glass in salute, and Bel could only laugh and shake her head. If by that little shift he had hoped to attach her to the group, he succeeded. One of the party spoke to her, and she had to answer, and it would be a few minutes now before she could get away somewhere safer.

Meanwhile, Jake was standing far too close to her. The room was cool, almost chilly, in anticipation of lots of body heat being generated, and she figured Jake would contribute his share. The temperature differential between him and the air made her shiver.

"Like to go outside?" he asked her. One wall of the room was glass, overlooking a beautifully designed terrace built on several levels, with a waterfall. The big doors were open, and people were being drawn into the late sunshine. "It's probably warmer in the sun."

"Sure," said Bel in her most matter-of-fact tone, but the fact that he had picked up on her discomfort made her bite her lip, and when he moved just that little bit closer she felt as if an invisible wave had struck her. She supposed distantly that was what a shock wave was. She twitched, betraying the responsive spasm in her muscles, and heard him swear softly.

"You are too damned attractive," he said. He was almost relieved when Bel stepped away.

The fact was, he had said what he said in the car out of sheer bravado, more than half expecting her to laugh at his declaration of their mutual attraction and assure him she couldn't stand him. Now that she had admitted that she was avoiding him not because she wasn't attracted, but because she *was,* he was on the edge of losing control with her.

Hell, with her I probably could take a realistic stab at forever.

He realized with uncomfortable abruptness where his thoughts were leading him. Next thing he knew, he'd be promising her the future! Which just showed how desperate a man could get, because he knew damned well roving was in his blood. His grandfather had made a misery of two women's lives trying to be what he was not. And Jake knew he was just like his grandfather. And his parents were still married only because his mother was prepared to forgive over and over again.

But for the first time he understood that maybe not every man who lied to a woman about his intentions did so in cold blood. It was easy to delude yourself when you really wanted something—and he guessed maybe he was no exception.

Your grandfather told me he loved her in a way he'd never loved me, and that if he married her he knew he'd be true to her all his life, but that if he stayed married to me he'd make us both unhappy. Well, I let him go—but she was as miserable with him as I'd ever have been. He didn't stay true to her longer than a month. He never did know himself for the kind of man he was.

Jake had always figured, hearing that story, that maybe his grandfather did know himself, and had deliberately misled both women about his intentions. And he'd lived in such different times, maybe there was an excuse for him.

But now he wondered. Maybe the only difference between him and the old womanizer had been that Jake had never before wanted a woman enough to start lying to himself.

Three

Bel had eaten almost nothing all day, and her first few sips of the Dom Pérignon, combined as it was with the heat of Jake's admiration, went straight to her head. Climbing beside him up the rocky steps that led along the banks of the beautiful little waterfall—man-made, but oh, so cleverly contrived to look like ideal nature!—she stumbled slightly.

She recovered from the stumble almost before it began. But instantly his hand moved to her waist, as if he had been waiting for the excuse. And it was only when he touched her that the champagne splashed out of her glass. Bel sucked in a little breath, and they both gazed down at her hand, as though the droplets of pale golden liquid lying on her flesh held some deep secret that had been puzzling mankind for millennia.

Which one of them had trembled so violently at the touch? Or was it each one?

Pause. His hand against her back, his immaculate white shirtfront so close to her, the curve of his neck and shoulder just on a level with her hungry cheek...a deep, deep longing to tuck her head into that very curve seemed to have been programmed into her from birth.

She could smell him. Smell was always powerful with her—the smell of wet dandelions would bring back a summer day when she was five with singing clarity. The smell of Jake, musky, male, with the undertone of an aftershave that she had never smelled before and would never now forget, took her to a time she could not place, touched off an unknown memory of perfection, triggered a yearning that was almost unbearable.

She did not dare to look up. To look into his face would be to invite his kiss, and to invite his kiss now would be a promise.

A promise to him...and to herself.

She had already made herself a very different promise. A promise that excluded the kind of choice that now faced her. Shakily refusing to lift her eyes, Bel took her glass into her right hand, lifted the left to her mouth and quickly sucked off the splashes of champagne.

"Cut that out!" Jake ordered furiously. "What are you trying to do? Prove something?"

Now, very startled, she did look up.

"I've never grabbed a woman who said no in my life!" he told her between clenched teeth. "And I am not going to start with you!"

His eyes were burning black, a phenomenon she noted with distant surprise. She had heard of white heat, yellow heat and red heat, all in some long-ago science class, but black heat? That was new. Maybe she should ask Tallia. She was the science brain of the family.

"Sorry," she muttered. "I didn't mean..."

"Yes, you damned well did!" His voice was low but biting. "Think I don't know the signs of a woman turned on by a man in rut? You make up your mind to come to me freely and willingly, and don't think I'll do the deciding for you!"

She stared at him helplessly. She really, really was out of her depth here.

His hand was on her upper arm, partly on soft green silk, partly on silky brown skin. "Do you want me to kiss you? Yes or no?"

His voice was low but full of passionate intensity. He was trembling. She felt responsive shivers course over her skin. Of course she could not let him kiss her now. The place was full of people. This was her sister's wedding. And if he started, where would he end?

"No," she lied.

"Then stop coming on like Eve with the apple!" he ordered her brutally, and because he knew that, whatever he said, he was within a micromillimetre of grabbing her and kissing her till she stopped saying a stupid no that she did not mean, Jake dropped his hand, turned and strode down the steps away from her.

He was panting like a hunted animal, a fact that infuriated him. And it didn't help his mood one iota to see that that damned, brainless woman in the blue hat was twinkling and smiling at him as though they were partners in some conspiracy and he had just flawlessly executed Stage C.

They had to sit beside each other at the head table. Bel supposed she had agreed to that in some long-ago planning session when she had felt invincible and had forgotten how much alcohol would be flowing. Now, although she was extremely tempted, she lacked the courage—or was it merely opportunity she lacked?—to switch the place cards.

She could see that Jake wasn't too thrilled, either. But a quick glance showed him her parents, and Brad's, making for the table, and he could hardly perform the switch under such interested eyes. Everybody would realize what he was doing and wonder why.

So Bel had to try to act as normal as possible, laugh and talk and contribute her mite to the occasion, when she was as nervous as a cat. Jake was clearly doing his best, too. In the desperate, foolish hope that alcohol might spread a haze over her anxiety, Bel began to swallow champagne in amounts previously unknown to her.

The food was delicious, and everybody was happy, and the champagne began to make her feel invulnerable to consequences. She laughed at everybody's jokes, more often than not sharing the moment with Jake. The table was round, and it was so easy to catch his eye, so difficult to look away...

What was virginity, in this day and age? What meaning did it have?

When the meal was eaten, and another round of champagne had been poured for the toasts, Jake groped in his pocket for his cue cards and slowly rose to his feet.

The room fell expectantly silent.

"Some of you know that Brad and I go back a long time," he began. "Almost thirty years, in fact. We met on the first day of kindergarten, out by the jungle bars, when a little blue-eyed feminist, whose name has disappeared down the years, was giving him grief over whose turn it was to cross the rope bridge." Jake paused.

"In case there can be any doubt on the subject, she said it was her turn."

The guests laughed gently, relaxing in the way groups

do when they know they are in the hands of a capable speaker.

Jake wished he could relax, too. He usually did feel comfortable making after-dinner speeches, but not this one. He was too well aware of what was coming—a whole lot of jokes about Brad's betrayal of the bachelor state, of Jake being forced, as a member of an exclusive club, to strip Brad of his badges…

He didn't want to say all those things, not now, not with Bel sitting right there gazing up at him. He wasn't even sure why he'd written them, unless it was some kind of defence mechanism.

But he knew he wasn't capable of the mental dexterity tonight that would be required to change it. He was experienced at reading his audience and changing his speech on the fly, adjusting to their reactions, whether judge, jury, or a mellow dinner audience. But tonight he had had too much to drink, and what was worse, his brain was fogged with a sexual and emotional intensity he didn't recall ever feeling, and certainly never before while fully dressed and in a public place.

He could get the speech out as he planned it, his memory forced by the cryptic notes on his cards. He could maybe tone it down some. But his brain just lacked the inventiveness, the flexibility he would have needed to change the tenor of it completely. He blundered on with deceptive smoothness. His audience was enjoying the speech.

"Brad and I were ten when we solemnly agreed that girls played pretty good baseball but were otherwise useless. We didn't come to this conclusion hastily, let me assure you. We spent several confused sessions trying to figure out some logical reason why God had invented them…well, we found out soon enough." Laughter.

"But it won't surprise you to hear that it wasn't logic that led us to the discovery."

More laughter. Bel, too, but he was digging his grave here. Of course she knew the truth already, but still he was sorry it had to be told so blatantly.

He took them through adolescence, and the great discovery of meaning in God's mysterious ways vis-à-vis women. And then one or two of his and Brad's less outrageous escapades, fit for consumption for all ages.

And then he got to the formation of the SWOF club.

"The letters stood for Sowing Wild Oats Forever," he informed them gravely. Of course he had edited that for public consumption. "Membership in this exclusive club had only two prerequisites—one, that the prospective member had never gone steady with a girl, and two, that he would swear never to do so."

There was a pregnant pause while Jake turned and sombrely gazed down at the defaulting member of the SWOF club. People laughed uproariously. When the laughter died down, he said, "I suppose it goes without saying that Brad has now been blackballed by the remaining members in good standing of the SWOF club." He told them how Brad's nemesis had entered his life, told them how he had tried to warn Brad of his danger...but all in vain. "And ladies and gentleman, tonight I have the unpleasant duty of removing Brad's name from the list of members...."

They loved it. It was ridiculous, it was lighthearted, and since no one had the least doubt that Brad Slinger was head-over-heels in love with his bride and Jake approved, it could offend no one.

Except Bel, who was smiling, and even laughing, but whose eyes had gone grave. She flashed a look at Jake once as he spoke, and then kept her eyes on her champagne glass. But the one look was enough. He had seen that look that night they had eaten dinner together and he had tried his games on her....

Of course he had planned a rider at the end. Of course he said, ''But seriously, now, I want to say how happy I am for Brad. I have never seen him happier....'' But though it meant something to the rest of his audience, he got a flick from Bel's eyes that told him what she thought of this about-face.

He got through it, proposed the toast, then sat down to very warm applause and laughter. He had done what he meant to do.

But he knew he had sounded like an immature jerk. Like just what he probably was—a man who couldn't face the thought of settling down and resented it when his friends fell by the wayside....

Bel knew better than to take it very seriously. It was clear Jake was an accomplished speaker and knew how to play to an audience, and she didn't waste time imagining that the SWOF club had ever existed except as a short-lived joke when Brad and Jake and their friends had been young and drunk.

But still, the underlying message was there. There had been none of that conventional my-turn-may-be-next stuff in the speech. He hadn't said anything about hoping he would be as lucky as Brad when his turn came. Nothing had changed, and she was a fool if she had been expecting it. He was not the marrying kind, he had told her. Whenever—if ever!—she made love to Jake Drummond, she could expect him to kiss her goodbye in the morning.

''Dance, Annabel?''

The bride and groom were whirling around the floor, and slowly other couples were joining them. Jake was on his feet, bending over her, before she guessed his intention.

She tried to steel herself to refuse, but before the thought had even formed she was standing up.

"I don't know whether that was sheer conditioned response, or what!" she said, when, on the dance floor, he turned and put his arm around her. Obediently she put her hand in his and of their own accord her feet began to follow him as he led her into the dance.

He didn't pretend not to understand. "It was *what*," he joked.

"You're dangerous," she said dreamily, as, responding to his touch, she tucked her head exactly where it wanted to go, in against his neck. She felt a little dizzy. She really must have drunk an awful lot.

"I'm glad you think so."

She lifted her head and looked into his face. "You are?"

"Sure. It does a man's ego a power of good to be thought dangerous. Especially when it's not true." He said that as if he meant himself.

"And it's not true with you?" she asked disbelievingly.

He laughed a little; she felt it ripple in his chest as he drew her head in against his throat again. She was being held very close. "No, it's not true with me."

His thighs were firm and hard and the pressure of them against hers was making her melt. Not dangerous? Her arm was around his shoulder, and she moved her hand just slightly, hoping he wouldn't notice, to touch the hair at the nape of his neck. It was thick but silky. Her forehead rested against his jaw, her breasts gently pressed against his chest.

"I think it is."

"You must have a very broad definition of dangerous."

"There are different kinds of danger."

"Ah! And what kind do I represent?"

"The love-'em-and-leave-'em kind," said Bel.

He was silent.

She lifted her head again. "Don't you?"

He took a breath and smiled into her eyes. "Have you heard that old story about the glass of water?"

She frowned. "Ye-es," she drawled suspiciously.

"Your problem is the same as someone who says the glass is half empty."

"It is?"

"You're thinking of the leave-'em part of the equation. It would be a lot more productive to concentrate on the love-'em."

She couldn't help the laughter that bubbled up in her.

"Productive for whom?"

"You and me," he said, sounding surprised. "Who else are we talking about?"

Her stomach did a neat back flip and, like wind over a pond, the entire surface of her skin rippled with sensation.

"No, I meant—" She couldn't have described exactly why his answer hit her so squarely. By her question she had meant—*you* or *me?* Jake's answer—he did not stress the *and*—seemed to say that his own mind-set did not even consider the possibility of there being an either-or between them when it came to sexual enjoyment.

He smiled, and the thought crossed her mind that he had gotten himself well under control since that moment on the terrace and was trying a different tactic with her.

"What did you mean?"

"I meant—productive for you or for me?"

He laughed aloud, so that several of the dancers near them turned their heads. Jake tilted his head to keep his words private. "You really have had some choice lovers, haven't you?" he murmured.

There was no answer to that, so she just looked at him.

"That isn't my first concern, anyway," she said, back-tracking, when he simply waited for her answer.

"Well, maybe it should be. What is your first concern?"

"I've told you. The half-empty glass."

He nodded slowly, taking it in. "How many men have loved you and left you, Bel?"

She knew it would be better to tell a lie, but she was afraid of looking like a fool if she was found out. "None," she admitted. "But—"

"None!" he repeated in surprise. "Who breaks off your relationships, you or the guy?"

"Well, but—"

"Come on, the truth, now!"

The truth was, she had broken off with two different men because, far from trying to persuade her to bed, they had approved of her stand and wanted to marry her. And she hadn't loved either of them enough to marry them.

But that wasn't what Jake meant.

And it was beyond her to explain to him that she had never had a sexual relationship and had therefore never been loved and left in the way they were talking about.

"Who gave who the bum's rush?"

"It wasn't like that!" she protested.

"You have given how many guys the heave-ho, Bel?" he persisted.

"Only two, and they were both fine, except I didn't want to marry them!" she cried, goaded.

Jake threw back his head and laughed, long and rich and deep.

Four

The tables were empty, the dance floor deserted.

"Is this the tenth time we've heard this love song?" Bel asked.

"I don't know. Why?"

"If it is, I'm learnin' the blues."

She was not sober, no way was she sober. But then again, was she drunk? When the music ended, Bel made the supreme effort and pushed herself upright, standing away from Jake's chest. She swayed. Definitely not stone cold sober. She gazed at the band as they began stowing their instruments.

"The mushis—musicians are quitting. Why are they quitting?"

"The last time I tipped them, they said it was the last time."

"Everybody else has gone! Where did they go?" Bel exclaimed in amazement, looking around.

They had danced almost exclusively with each other through the latter half of the evening. For the last hour, when they and two other couples had the floor to themselves, the band had played slow dances. Now, except for the members of the band, who were packing up, they were alone.

She'd never felt so at one with someone in her life. Never felt such a strong, sweet power of need flow through her—a vital liquid with its own set of vessels through her system. His chest, his mouth, his hands, his thighs, his voice, his eyes... If you could fall in love with a man dancing, Bel reflected, that was what she had done.

But of course you couldn't. She hadn't.

"They have gone where most good little boys and girls go—and even more bad ones," Jake informed her with a seductive smile pulling at his lips. "To bed."

Good thing she would be sober tomorrow. Things would look different then.

"It must be late," she observed sagely.

Jake laughed softly. "It must be," he agreed.

If everyone was gone, she was at risk. She was safe with Jake only in company, she knew that much.

"Time to get outta here!" she muttered.

She led the way back to their table in the empty room. They had been moved to a small table at the edge of the dance floor, specially brought in for the purpose, so the staff could clear and dismantle the other tables. All the big tables were gone now, the darkened room nearly empty.

"Have you got your key? What's your room number?"

Oh, thank goodness she had had such forethought! If she had had a room booked, and Jake took her to it...well, you didn't need to be Psychic Sally to guess what would happen...

"I'm going home," said Bel, catching a smile from the saxophonist as he wiped down his sax.

"Home?" Jake raised his eyebrows. "How are you going to do that?"

She smiled her triumph. "I brought a car here yest—" she paused, frowning. "Was it yesterday?"

"Whenever it was, you can't drive now."

Clutching her handbag and her bouquet, Bel straightened, blinking. Well, here it came. The hard sell. "Why not?" she demanded, just a little defiantly, in expectation of having to resist pressure.

"Bel, you aren't sober."

"I'm not drunk." She yawned widely. "I'd know if I was drunk."

"And you're asleep on your feet."

"No, I'm not." No, she wasn't. She was only too awake, and alive. Her head was stupid, but her body—oh, her body yearned for the touch of Jake's again. His arms, his thighs...oh boy. She was an electric guitar, all plugged in and humming, waiting to be played by a master. Bel clutched the bouquet to her breast. "I'll be fine."

He followed her silently as she walked out into the lighted foyer of the hotel and approached the bellman's desk with the faintest weave in her step. Defiantly she rang a little bell, and when a man appeared from an office behind, she handed him a small square of plastic.

"Could you have my car brought around, please?"

"Certainly, miss." Turning to the phone on the desk, he lifted the receiver, then raised his eyes to Jake. "You'll be driving, I take it, sir?"

Jake, his hands in his pockets, shook his head in a firm negative.

"Ah." Back went the receiver into the cradle. "Miss, do you think you're perhaps a little tired?"

"Course I'm tired. That's why I'm goin' home! To bed." She yawned again.

"I wonder if you wouldn't rather stay in the hotel for what's left of the night."

Was the man crazy? If there was one thing Bel knew, it was that if she stayed in the hotel for what was left of the night—and however much was left, she knew it was enough—she would spend it in Jake's bed.

"No, I have to go home," she said resolutely.

"I'm sorry to say this, miss, but we have a policy at the hotel that requires you to take a Breathalyzer before I can bring your car. Would you care to step into the office?"

She was so aware of Jake lurking there behind her, his body heat surrounding her. Her blood was rushing. She whirled. "What did you tell him? I'm not drunk!"

Jake lifted his shoulders in an expressive shrug. "If you're not, the Breathalyzer will show it and this man will give you your keys."

"I can't be drunk! I have to go home!"

She stumbled after the bellman into the office, blew hard into his little machine, and read the figure for herself. She let out a long, hopeless wail. "But I stopped drinking ages ago!"

"Alcohol does take time to clear the system, miss," the bellman said apologetically. "Would you like me to get you a taxi?"

"A taxi!" She breathed again. "Yes—oh!" She looked at her little bag. "How much would a taxi cost to Vancouver?"

"To *Vancouver*? Well, it would cost a very substantial amount, miss—I would say, between seventy and a hundred dollars—that is, if I could find someone willing to make the journey at this hour."

"A hundred dollars! But I'm a student!" she exclaimed

stupidly. She didn't have a hundred dollars, and her credit cards—she'd left everything at her parents' house. Which was filled to the rafters with guests, all of whom would be sound asleep. She should have left much earlier, as planned, changed at the house, and then set off for her own apartment in Vancouver at a reasonable hour...but she'd been enjoying herself too much dancing—with Jake.

"You'll look after her, Jake?" she vaguely remembered her mother asking when she had drunkenly stated her decision to continue dancing for a while. Look after her? Hah!

And there he was, still waiting, when she returned to the lobby.

"I am going to get a room for the night," Bel announced loftily. She realized dimly that a room in this understated palace would set her back a lot more than a mere hundred. What a fool she had been! It was all the champagne's fault. The champagne, and Jake's eyes, she amended.

"I've already asked. There isn't one available. The place is stuffed to the gills with Brad's guests," said Jake.

"Oh. Oh boy, oh boy, oh boy!" Bel gazed at him, her eyes widening, feeling like a mouse with a snake. "What am I going to do?" she asked faintly.

Jake looked at her impassively, his hands in his pockets. "You have two choices. You can sit it out in the TV room, with another homeless inebriate wedding guest who's already snoring there, or you can come to my room."

Why does the devil look so attractive when he's offering you loaded choices? Bel wondered.

"I've got a very big bed. Plenty of room for two," said Jake, leading her resistlessly to the elevator.

It was the sort of hotel that put two luxurious terry-cloth bathrobes on the back of the bathroom door, one black and one white. It also had every cosmetic aid imaginable on the broad marble sink. Feeling woozier with every moment that passed, Bel locked the door, took off her dress and stockings. This left her in her pale green silk underwear, of which there wasn't nearly enough.

She removed her makeup with a careless hand and some delicious-smelling cream, washed her face, and stared at herself in the huge mirror. The delicate green silk bra and briefs, specially chosen for the day, wrapped firm breasts, neat waist and hips. Her softly tanned body curved in all the right places, her legs were almost as good as Tallia's.

"This is it," she muttered. "You won't be the same after tonight. You won't be a virgin anymore." She wasn't a fool. When a man like Jake was determined to seduce you, and you got undressed and got into his bed…she knew what was coming. She would be no match for his practiced seduction, because she melted when he even looked at her. And she wasn't sober, and just the thought of him undressing on the other side of the door made her burn with excitement.

Well, it was no good pretending she hadn't gotten herself into this. She should never have allowed herself to dance with him like that, pressing up against him, letting him kiss her neck, stroke her bare upper arm.… She shivered with pleasure at the memory.

Maybe she had deliberately engineered it. Maybe unconsciously she wanted to give in to Jake, whatever the future cost.

Would she look different tomorrow? They said people could tell, but she knew that wasn't true, because if it were, an expert like Jake would have known.

Should she tell him in advance? She sort of knew what to do—like everybody else her age she'd had a pretty relentless training from Hollywood movies. But still, as with any skill, there must be a big difference between theory and practice.

How could she tell him? *Jake, I'm a little short on practical experience here?* Or *I haven't got much hands-on experience?*

Bel giggled and it turned into a hiccup.

She was feeling woozier by the minute. How could that be—that you got progressively drunker even when you'd stopped drinking? The bright lights all around the mirror were hurting her eyes. Bel turned and reached for a bathrobe.

She chose the black one, to give her confidence and so as not to look too much like the virgin she was. And also to prevent Jake wearing it and looking even more like a handsome devil.

She wrapped it tightly around herself and secured it with the belt. It reached the floor. Then she picked up her dress and took a deep breath and, stockings trailing out of her arms, opened the door into the big bedroom.

Jake was standing at the foot of the bed, bent over a small overnight case. He had taken off his jacket, shirt and tie, and his shoes and socks, but he was still wearing the black formal trousers with the strip of ribbon down the sides. As she came in he straightened, closed the case and tossed something onto the bed.

Bel closed her eyes. He did not need the help of a black bathrobe. He was the sexiest, most attractive man she'd ever seen. The room reeled and she quickly opened her eyes again.

The bed was softly lighted, the rest of the room in darkness. The maid had turned down the bed long ago, but the little chocolates she had left on the pillows had been removed by Jake to the wooden surround that curved around the bed and served as headboard and bedside tables.

He was smiling, coming around the bed towards her. "Feeling a bit woozy?" he asked solicitously.

Her heart thumped crazily in her breast. "A little."

Gently he took her dress from her and hung it on a hanger, picked up her cobweb stockings. He laid them over the back of a chair. The thing he had tossed onto the bed was a pale green polo shirt.

"Oh, good," she said. "We match."

Jake turned with that seductive smile and ran his eyes all over her, bundled up in the bathrobe. "Your flowers, you mean?"

Bel blinked. "What?"

"You still have flowers in your hair."

He approached her, and she sank helplessly down to sit on the bed, her eyes wide and dark as she gazed up at him. With what seemed to her like cool expertise, he slipped his fingers into her hair and began to search for the pins that held the flowers.

It felt as if honey flowed from his touch all over her skin. Warm, sweet sensation that was delicious to her senses. Bel bit her lip and closed her eyes. His touch made even the tips of her hair tingle. Her hair suddenly fell down around her shoulders, and she gasped.

"There." She opened her eyes again. He had the little wreath of flowers in his hand, and there were hairpins scattered under the lamp on the bedside table.

She swallowed.

"Stand up," he commanded.

She swayed as she did so, partly from drunkenness, partly from nerves. Jake put his hands on the collar of her bathrobe and began to slip it off her shoulders. She took a deep breath. So this was it.

He looked at her long brown body as it was revealed and his jaw clenched. "Turn around."

His hands expertly released the catch of her bra, and she felt cool air on her breasts. Jake bent forward from behind her, extending an arm to drop the bra on the bed, and she held her breath for the touch of his hands.

"Jake, I—I think I should tell you—"

"Lift up your arms," he said.

"What?"

He was holding up the polo shirt. "So I can put this on you."

Dumbly obedient, she held up her arms. He fitted his polo shirt over her hands, pulled it down over her head, gently eased her hair from its folds. Then he bent down and lifted the sheet.

"Get in."

She crawled in between cool sheets, her skin leaping with every contact, and laid her head on the pillow. "Jake, I—"

He covered her and, bending down, kissed her on the mouth. She smiled up at him, melted by the taste of him, her hands of their own accord reaching up to press his warm furry chest.

"Jake, maybe I should tell you—"

"In a minute," he said, straightening. He reached out a hand and flicked off the lamp. Her side of the bed was in gloom. Only the small soft pool of light on the other side of the wide bed prevented complete darkness.

He melted away into the bathroom. She heard the sound of running water for a moment. Then the thick door clicked shut, and there was only silence.

Five

Suddenly she was awake, staring with wide-open eyes at an unfamiliar wall. She knew where she was, she had not forgotten it even in sleep: she had spent the night with Jake Drummond in a hotel. She lay still, trying to sense if he was asleep or awake beside her.

She could remember everything—the champagne, the slow dancing, the car, her decision, Jake holding the sheet while she slipped into the big bed....

The only thing she could not remember was his love-making. Bel shut her eyes and drew in a long, trembling breath. Was this the end of all those years of struggle and determination? She had been too drunk to remember the most important moment of her adult life to date?

Surely if she lay quietly for a moment, it would all come back to her, the way dreams sometimes did. Bel lay motionless, waiting for remembrance to slither through the latticework of forgetfulness. The sun was shining behind the blinds with a pale lack of intensity that seemed appropriate to the moment.

No memory surfaced. A little snort of laughter escaped her. Was that sex, then? Less memorable even than dancing? What a lot of fuss over nothing! She stifled her cynical amusement for fear of waking Jake with it.

Goodness, what would she say to him? What *could* she say? She had heard of faking orgasm, but this was ridiculous! She wasn't going to invent enthusiasm for something on which she drew a complete mental blank.

She heaved a sigh. She supposed she would have to confess that her drunken mind had chosen not to record the event. Would she pretend not to remember anything else, either, to save his feelings? Say her life was a blank from the middle of the evening on?

Oh, what a mess! Who would have guessed such a thing could be possible?

Maybe if she got a look at his sleeping face she would start to remember something. In any case, she couldn't lie here forever, afraid to move. The situation wasn't going to go away. Slowly, slowly, Bel began to inch over onto her back, hoping not to wake him. At last she was able to look over.

She was alone. The other side of the bed was completely undisturbed, the quilted spread lying smooth and flat over the mattress, curving neatly over the pillows.

"Thanks," Jake muttered to the waitress as, with a cheery, innocent smile, she filled his coffee cup.

"Can I take your order, sir?"

He lifted one hand in a negative, and she smiled more broadly, recognizing one who needed time to wake up. "I'll just leave the menu with you," she said, wrinkling her nose conspiratorially, and whisked away, leaving the trace of a crisp young perfume on the air. His nose automatically identified it: Rebel.

Perfume had always been a good starter with women, in his college days. ''Mmm, Rebel,'' he would say to a woman with a resigned smile, shaking his head. And when she demanded to know what he meant, he would wonder helplessly why any woman he fell for across the room always turned out to wear Rebel.

Or Patchouli, or Femme, or Opium, or Poison. Or any of a couple of dozen perfumes he could still unerringly identify, even though he hadn't used the technique since his professional career began. It had never failed to entice a woman into conversation, and that, of course, was half the battle.

He wondered what perfume Bel wore. He had never actually clocked it, though he found her scent heady enough. Too damned heady.

All around him the tables were filling up with wedding guests, looking more or less the worse for wear. He nodded to those who caught his eye as he drank his coffee, but he was in no mood for social conversation, and by the look of them, neither was anyone else. There had been a heavy flow of champagne last night, a very generously stocked bar.

With Bel he had forgotten all his expertise—in fact, he had come out with some really dumb stuff that appalled him. *What's the point of arguing a woman into bed?* he used to say to less capable friends. *She won't be happy when she gets there, and neither will you.* But she had ended up where he wanted her, in the end, in spite of his unprecedented clumsiness. And then…and then he hadn't done anything about it. He had put her to bed like a child and spent the night on a damned uncomfortable sofa.

He finished the coffee in his cup and waved for more.

The pretty girl wearing Rebel, who was probably anything but, obligingly swooped.

"There you go!" she said bracingly.

There he went.

What the hell was the matter with him? He had to get a grip on life. Something was happening with him. He didn't know what it was, but he sure didn't like it.

"Hi."

Jake looked up so quickly he almost spilled his coffee. Bel was standing there, looking sheepish, in last night's party dress, her hair falling softly over her bare shoulders.

"Hi." He stood as she pulled out the chair, and they both sat down.

"I got your note," she informed him. He had left a scrawl telling her he was in the hotel café, on a Post-it note stuck to the bathroom mirror

"How're you feeling?" he asked.

"Pretty good, considering the amount of fizz I must have put away last night," Bel returned with a smile. "How about you?"

"Not bad." He was wearing his ruffled formal shirt with a pair of well-worn jeans, probably because he had given her his only casual top last night.

"That sofa must have been uncomfortable for a man of your height," she murmured, then glanced up with a smile as the Rebel approached with her coffeepot. "Thank you," Bel told her, accepting a menu. She glanced down at it. She was ravenous. "I'll have the breakfast special, please."

"Bacon, sausages or ham?"

"Bacon, thanks."

"Waffles or pancakes?"

"Ummm—pancakes."

"What about you, sir? Are you ready to order now?"

"Bring me the same."

As the waitress departed Bel lifted her coffee cup and smiled quizzically at Jake over it. Saying nothing, she took a tentative sip, then another, then set down her cup.

"I *am* right in thinking you slept on the sofa?"

He nodded.

Bel's face lost its smile and she dropped her eyes to her coffee cup. "Sometimes the pursuit must be the most interesting part," she supposed softly. She was smiling, but it did hurt. He had spent all that time arguing with her, telling her what they had was so special...

"Bel, you were drunk."

At that, she looked up with an incredulous smile. "Are you telling me you've never made love with a partner in a state of inebriation before?"

"No, I'm not telling you that. But it is a very long time since I deliberately took advantage of a woman's drunken state."

She raised her eyebrows.

"There are rules about that, you know," he said.

"Even for you?"

"What kind of a crack is that? Where did you get the idea that I'm a monster?"

Bel shrugged and absently spooned more sugar into her coffee, then sat there stirring it.

"I wasn't that drunk."

"You were over the drink-sex limit," he said, with a smile.

Bel laughed a little and shook her head. "There's a drink-sex limit? Not that I ever heard of!"

He shook his head. "You really have had some wow experiences, haven't you?"

Her eyes flashed. "No one has *ever* gotten me drunk and then...and then..."

"Well, then, you should be grateful you can still say that this morning."

Bel gasped. He was talking as if she were *complaining* because he hadn't taken advantage of her!

She clenched her jaw. "I am. *Very* grateful. Do you think I would *complain* because you didn't...?"

There was a glint in his eyes. He shrugged. "It kind of sounded like it," he said.

"Well, I wasn't! All I was saying was—" She broke off.

The glint in his eyes now became apparent on his lips, and a corner of his mouth went up, as if he was trying to suppress a smile and couldn't quite.

"Yes?" he prompted. He was looking very sexy, like a French actor or something, but the fact that she could clock that in such a moment only made Bel angrier with herself. And with him.

"I just want to point out to you that it was all a line, what you were handing me yesterday. So please don't—" She stopped herself. She had been going to say *don't try it on me again,* but it occurred to her that if he couldn't be bothered making love to her when he had her virtually naked in his bed, she didn't stand in very much danger of him trying *any* line on her in the future.

But of course that didn't disappoint her. It was a relief, in fact!

He didn't help her out by talking over her or anything like that, just waited till it was perfectly clear she wasn't going to go on. And then some.

Then suddenly his eyes lost that teasing smile and a look of naked intensity was revealed.

"Believe me, I'd be very happy to make up for my cretinous lapse of judgement on any day or night you care to name,'' he said. "Don't make the mistake of thinking that resisting you was easy, Bel, or ever would be for me.''

Bel caught her breath against the little puff of flame that his look ignited in her. She had taken a light, jokey mood and transformed it into something dangerously volatile. Was that what they meant by *playing with fire?* She sat up straight and shook her head involuntarily.

"Sorry, I shouldn't have—I mean, it's hard to explain, but I d-don't—'' she stammered.

He leaned over. "No, it is not hard to explain,'' and his teeth flashed now in a smile that was anything but friendly. "You said you didn't want me, Bel, because you want commitment. I respected that last night, and now you're blaming me. But remember what I told you yesterday—I don't rape anybody, and never have. You keep trying to tantalize me, and then you say no.''

"I don't—''

"Yes, you do. You're acting like a Victorian virgin, Bel, and all I can say is, if that's your technique, it's no wonder you get such lousy lovers, because any man who wants a woman against her will has got problems.''

She sat up straight, furious. "Jake, I do not—''

"Then don't come on to me again unless you mean it!'' he said, in a gritty kind of voice, his eyes narrowed, his forefinger raised and punching the air in front of her nose in a gesture that made her feel like a witness committing perjury.

The Rebel approached with two plates full of perfectly cooked food, but her face lost its smile as Jake got to his feet. "Sorry, I've been called to the office,'' he said, reaching into his pocket for his cash and peeling off a couple of twenties.

"Aren't you going to eat first?'' the girl asked in dismay, proving that she was another one looking forward to wedding bells and babies and a man she could feed up and make healthy and happy.

"Call me when you make up your mind," he said to Bel, dropped the twenties onto the table, and with a last nod, turned on his heel and strode off.

"But it's Sunday!" the waitress muttered, still staring after him, forlornly clutching his plate.

"He's a very dedicated worker," Bel told her.

The car she was driving was actually Tallia's car, which the two girls had driven to their parents' house the day before the wedding. The gorgeous, low-slung, turquoise sports car had been one of Brad's first gifts to Tallia after she moved into his penthouse, and Bel loved it almost as much as Tal did.

She whirled along the mountain's curves and thought how awful it would have been if she had been allowed her way last night and as a result had crashed this lovely car. And that wasn't even counting what might have happened to her own skin. She would phone the hotel manager when she got back home and ask him to thank the bellman.

She wondered if Jake would have forcibly stopped her if the bellman hadn't. If he had, she would certainly have considered it deliberate manipulation on his part.

But she would have been wrong.

Was it true, what he had told her? Or was there some other explanation—like, he was only interested in pursuit and she had proved too easy in the end? Or maybe he had seen her naked and just hadn't been turned on by what he saw. Or—but there wasn't any point in thinking about it. He had said he wouldn't call her, and she believed that.

And since she would never call him, they weren't likely to see much of each other. It would be easy for her to ask

Tallia not to invite them both together unless it was a large party.

She should be glad of all this. She *was* glad. But she was also aware of a feeling of discomfort, or dissatisfaction. Was he right? Did she just want the decision taken out of her hands? She had never acted that way before. When she was explaining herself to Nat and Will she hadn't been accused of any tricks.

But then, she hadn't been all that sexually attracted to Nat or Will. She had liked being held and kissed and caressed, but she had had no difficulty in knowing exactly where the line lay. Or enforcing it.

She had read and heard and watched a lot of film that said this wild kind of sexual attraction happened, but although she'd dreamed, she guessed now that she hadn't really believed it. She hadn't realized that such a thing could affect the way you behaved and thought. She had imagined that she would go on dating men like Nat and Will until there was one who—what?—one whom she knew she could marry.

But she hadn't ever imagined that she would be so torn by conflicting needs and desires. Nor had she ever given serious consideration to the possibility that when she finally felt serious about a guy he would not be interested.

She'd been spoiled by Nat and Will, who had fallen in love with her. She'd never thought about being on the other end of the equation. Of course she had realized it might happen that she would get hurt, that she would start a sexual relationship with someone she loved and that it would eventually go sour...but that she would be faced with the choice of deliberately entering a short-term affair with a man who wasn't half as attracted as she was...she had no contingency plans for this scenario.

She had just never counted on meeting someone like Jake Drummond.

Most of her parents' guests were still milling around when she arrived at the house, and Bel changed and spent a couple of hours helping her mother make lunch and then visiting with relatives she didn't see all that often. The Harrises had come in force from Toronto, and most of the Loves had come, too.

Lunch was served as a buffet, and people sat all over the lawn to take advantage of another fabulous day. Bel sank down on a soft green patch of grass in the bright sunshine, and within a couple of minutes her Aunt Miranda, that notorious matchmaker, settled herself comfortably and purposefully beside her.

Bel laughed aloud.

"Aw, Aunt Miranda, don't tell me I'm on your hit list already! I only just finished writing my finals! Give a girl a break!"

"Now, Bel, you're being silly," her aunt said tolerantly. "I'm certainly not going to try to push any man at *you* today."

"Really?" Bel asked dubiously.

"Of course not. There's no need to. You've already found someone, and I hear he's *very* eligible!"

Bel chewed a bit of sandwich, staring at her aunt.

"Who?" she asked faintly.

"That absolutely gorgeous hunk you were climbing into on the dance floor all night, who else?" said Aunt Miranda. Aunt Miranda had never quite left the sixties. "Jake Drummond. I hear he's a very successful lawyer with substantial investments."

Bel closed her eyes. "Who exactly did you third-degree about him, Aunt Miranda?"

"Jake's mother and I were at the same table, you know. She seemed very pleased to think Jake had found someone so nice. I told her all about you, of course. But she did warn me that he's had lots of girlfriends in the past, and I just—"

Bel interrupted firmly. "Aunt Miranda, Jake is not my boyfriend. We've never dated, and we aren't going to."

"What?" Miranda blinked. "Don't be silly, Bel, you didn't dance with anyone else!"

"Yes, I did, I danced with quite a few other men, early on, but I know what you mean, and it wasn't what it looked like."

"Do you mean to tell me you wasted all that energy on a one-night stand? I don't believe you!"

"I was drunk, Aunt Miranda, and whatever it looked like I did *not* sleep with him, and I am not his girlfriend, and we are not going to get married!" Bel said desperately. She couldn't *stand* it if her aunt started her matchmaking stuff with Jake. "Look, why don't you find me some nice suitable boy? It's time I settled down, don't you think?"

"But rogues do reform!" Aunt Miranda wailed. "And his mother told me that his grandfather—"

"Aunt Miranda."

"Yes, dear."

"No."

"But his mother told me things you might find helpful, Annabel."

"I already know all I need to know about Jake Drummond." Bel stuffed the last of her lunch into her mouth and leapt to her feet. "Thank you anyway." She dusted off her hands, bent to pick up her plate and glass, and with a wave slipped through the back door into the kitchen.

One of her brothers was grazing among the breaded

mushrooms. "Hell!" she exploded with all the pent-up emotion of the past few minutes.

Cyrus turned as she noisily stacked her dishes in the open dishwasher.

"Who have you had a run-in with?"

"Three guesses."

"Miranda."

"You can save those other two guesses for some deeper mystery, then."

"Well, little sister, if you will get drunk as a brandy pudding and spend the night superglued to the most eligible male at the party you have to expect to hear incipient wedding bells pealing over your head in the morning if your Aunt Miranda was present at the scene."

"I know, I know!" Bel examined the mushrooms, which were disappearing down his throat at a fair rate. "Are these that good? I didn't have any."

"Delicious. Aunt Whatsit's specialty. So, what's with you and the bridegroom's best friend?"

Bel chewed a mushroom and gazed at her brother. Although they were separated by more than eight years in age, there had always been a special closeness between them.

"He's a Casanova," she said.

Cyrus, turning to the grilled peppers for contrast, nodded. "Uh huh," he said encouragingly.

"Well, and I got too drunk to drive back last night—the hotel wouldn't give me my car keys. And there were no rooms available."

"Neat trick. I wonder how he managed all that." Realizing that this was going to be a serious talk, Cyrus straightened, turned, resting his hips against the table, popped a tidbit in his mouth, and crossed his arms, giving Bel his full attention.

"So I had a choice of Jake's room or sleeping it off in the television lounge," she said unnecessarily.

"You chose Jake's room, of course, and he had his wicked way with you and this morning—what happened this morning?"

"Yes, but Russ, he didn't."

Cyrus blinked. "Didn't what?" he asked in surprise. "Didn't go in for the kill?"

"He slept on the sofa."

He reached blindly behind him and picked up a tidbit at random, putting it absently into his mouth as he furrowed his brow, and chewed thoughtfully. "Interesting case. Why?"

"He *said,* because it's against the rules to take advantage when a girl is drunk."

"You tell me this guy's a Casanova?" Russ asked, powerful disbelief in his tone.

She nodded mutely.

"Doesn't add up."

"I know. So then—why didn't he, Russ?"

He rubbed his nose.

"You still a virgin, Bel?"

She nodded again.

"Well, some guys are scared of that, especially if they don't have serious intentions. Not many guys, of course— I guess by now you've had your fill of the ones who really enjoy collecting scalps, especially of women who make a thing of saving themselves for a significant relationship."

She nodded. "But it doesn't mean anything, because Jake doesn't know."

He smiled. "You sure about that?"

"Yes, he thinks I've...well, he definitely has no idea. So why, then?"

He picked up something from her tone, and gave her a level look. "You're sorry he didn't, huh?"

"Well, yes and no."

"Tired of virginity, Bel?"

She dropped her eyes and ate something at random. "No, it isn't that."

Cyrus took a deep, sympathetic breath and sighed it noisily out. "Hard luck, falling for a guy who spreads it around so thin."

"Yeah," she breathed, feeling the sudden burn of tears at the back of her throat.

For a moment there was silence between them, the silence of brotherly empathy.

Then, knowing his answer in advance, she said, "So was it just that he didn't—that he wasn't all that interested, Russ?"

"I don't know, Bel. From where I sat he was looking pretty damn interested all night long."

She knew she shouldn't allow herself to take comfort from that, but she couldn't help smiling through her tears.

"Oh, God, what a mess!" she exclaimed, wiping a hand over her face and sniffing loudly. "What should I do?"

"Bel, I hardly talked to the guy. It's just impossible for me to second-guess him here. Want me to phone him up and ask him his intentions?"

She laughed again. "What's your best guess, Russ?"

He shook his head thoughtfully, scratched his head, rubbed his chin. "My best guess is, he knows you're a virgin and is too decent a guy to mess with you when he's not serious."

"Mmm," she murmured softly. "What's your second-best guess?"

"A decent guy doesn't want to make the running because a woman was too drunk to say no—especially not if he really likes her. So my second-best guess is, he's more deeply involved than he's telling you. Or maybe than he knows himself.''

Bel covered her eyes with her hand, while her heartbeat soared with hope. "Oh, Russ!" she whispered. "Oh, if only you're right!''

Six

Jake drew the car to a stop and reached out to press the entry code. As the big gates clicked and whined open, he smoothly shifted into First and inched forward along the drive.

It was quite a house. Large, square and imposing, in red brick, with mullioned windows, it also had an all-weather swimming pool, tennis courts, and substantial outbuildings.

It wasn't his type of architecture; he preferred the Johnny Winterhawk design in cedar next door—which, he had noticed absently on the way in, was for sale. If he were buying, he'd be tempted. But he could see the appeal of this. And Tallia, looking ahead to a time when there would be children, was delighted she would have her lab and office right on the grounds. Brad was planning on doing a lot of working from home, too, he knew.

He parked the car beside the turquoise convertible. So

Bel was in. He had been half hoping she would be out on an errand. He went lightly up the steps to the front door and rang the bell.

He glanced around as he waited. The gardeners clearly knew their stuff, he noted with approval. The last time he had come the place had looked like a jungle, and they had quelled it without killing the attractive riot of colour and growth.

Bel was pretty efficient. He was in no doubt that she would have the whole place in perfect condition in time for the newlyweds' return.

When there was no answer, he didn't use his key, but went back down the steps and around to the back. The domed roof of the swimming pool was open and a giant hose was lying across the water. Something was humming away, so he guessed Bel had that in hand, too. He dropped his briefcase in a garden chair.

It was Jake who had suggested that Brad should hire Bel to oversee the redecoration while Brad and Tallia were on a prolonged honeymoon. It timed well with her finishing university—Tallia had mentioned one night that Bel would be at a loose end after writing her exams. Jake had seen it as a great opportunity for getting to know Bel while she was, so to speak, a captive audience. He was looking after the financial end of the renovations, so naturally he and Bel would have to confer a lot. And he could make sure that they conferred over dinner....

That had been before the wedding. Now he regretted his brainstorm. The newlyweds had been gone two weeks, and this was his first visit. He knew he should have been out here every day or two. He hardly even knew why he was avoiding meeting her. Maybe because every time they spoke on the phone he broke out in a cold sweat.

Nerves. He'd never suffered nerves around a woman in

his life. Well—his mother, when she'd caught him in some misdemeanour, but that didn't count. Nerves, and the conviction that if he was going to stick to his good intentions, the less he saw of temptation the better.

His presence hadn't really been essential, as it turned out. Bel seemed to be a natural manager. But it galled him to be so weak.

As he crossed the lawn he caught movement through a window in the newly redecorated building that Tallia had earmarked as her research lab. It was Bel. Jake stood still for a moment, then unconsciously moved closer, watching. Though the whole complex was now air conditioned, he knew, the windows were wide open to the warmth of the day.

She was unpacking a crate.

Her long brown hair was casually caught up in a large clip, from which one bunch escaped to form a fan on top of her head, and locks and tendrils fell against her cheeks and neck and down her back. It had been hastily done, simply to keep her hair from her face while she worked, but other women could spend hours in front of the mirror without achieving the erotic effect that this tousle had on his hormones.

It seemed to say he could undress her with one squeeze of that clip. He thought of her hair as it had been on the wedding night, falling down her back as he pulled out the flowers, and from there he remembered how he had unhooked her bra, and of course from there he thought of those proud, full brown breasts and how his hands had burned to stroke and hold them....

She was wearing a small short sundress that barely reached the middle of her thighs, and each time she bent over he caught sight of white cotton panties at the top of those long, curving legs.

He had had his chance, and he had blown it. But he knew that he had done the right thing. And he had to go on doing the right thing. Bel wanted forever, and he couldn't give it to her, even though right now he felt if he could make love to her just once he'd never need another woman as long as he lived. That was just hormones talking.

Unconsciously he moved closer.

The muscles played in her arms, too. She had probably worked out at the university gym, the way he had during his university days. Or maybe Brad had given her a lifetime membership to Fitness Now. Hell, or maybe she just enjoyed good, healthy, exuberant, vibrant, satisfying sex five times a day, the way he would like to with her. He wondered who the lucky guy was, and how much trouble he would have ousting the son of a...

No, he reminded himself firmly, he wasn't going to do that. If she had a relationship—from the way she talked the guy was a loser in bed, whatever else he was, but if that was what she wanted...

Boy, he sure would like to correct her impressions about how important sex was.

No.

Anyway, she had said she didn't want sex with Jake, not because she was in a relationship, but because she figured Jake wasn't in it for the long term.

Maybe she worked out after all.

Jake breathed a sigh of relief.

One of the little spaghetti straps had fallen down over one smooth arm, and she turned a little towards him, and now he could see the way her breasts shifted under the thin cotton as she picked up a hammer and bent to open another...

"Eeeeaaaaaagggghhhhh!!!"

The scream tore his reverie to shreds. As the hammer came whistling past his head, Jake jumped sideways, thereby narrowly avoiding extinction.

"What do you think you're doing, you screeching pervert?"

He froze. It was as if all connection between his motor brain and his body had been severed with her words. He stood there in mute helplessness, his eyes wide with surprise, staring at her as she ran to the window and leaned out.

"Jake!" Bel cried in amazement. "What on *earth* were you doing?"

Mercifully, his jaw engaged. "Ah...ah...sorry, Bel, I was just..." He lifted his hands feebly. Pity his brain hadn't engaged, too. "Just lookin' at you, kid," he tried, with what he knew was a stupid grin.

Her hands covered her cheeks in remembered horror. "God, I thought you were a peeper! You really gave me a horrible scare."

"Me, too," he said. "You've got a scream like a banshee, Bel. I'm grateful I didn't have a heart attack." He bent and straightened. "Would you like your hammer back? Sorry you can't inscribe my name on it, but ducking was kind of instinctive."

She took it and began to laugh. It was one of the things he'd instantly liked about her—her unashamed laugh. Today the release of shock gave it added impetus, and he couldn't help being drawn in. Then the two of them were suddenly bent double with laughter, Bel with her arms folded on the windowsill, her forehead resting on them, Jake leaning against the wall, his deep laughter booming out to mingle with hers.

After several helpless minutes, Bel lifted her head and

wiped the tears from her eyes. "Oh, how ridiculous!" she said, laughter still bubbling up. "Oh, your face!"

Women didn't often laugh at him. He found the experience unnerving, but then he was already totally unnerved by the whole of the last few minutes. Or maybe from the day he met Bel.

"Are you laughing at me?" he demanded.

More irrepressible laughter welled up in her. "Well, but Jake, what were you doing there, staring at me like a—?"

"What the hell, Bel, I caught sight of you through the window and stopped to look. You're an attractive woman," he argued, and inwardly cursed himself for the weakness of that. He was always on ice with her, it seemed. He was never able to get his footing. It was an entirely new experience, and the wonder of it was, he was still so crazily attracted to her. He would have thought, if he'd thought about the possibility of such a thing happening to him, that it would turn a man off.

He didn't want to make the connection that maybe he was unnerved *because* he was so crazily attracted to her.

"Do you normally watch attractive women through windows when you get the chance?" She was grinning. He could see there was no way to recover himself—he was going to go on putting his foot in it and she was going to go on laughing.

She was crazily sexy when she laughed—her breasts trembled behind the cotton that covered them, a lock of hair brushed against her cheek, and her mouth was wide and inviting.

He leaned in the window, and, forgetting all his firm intentions, put his hands on her ears, and kissed her full on her laughing mouth.

There was a sizzle in his nerves, as if two wires carrying a huge voltage had touched. He had meant it to be a simple kiss, just a little friendly something to shut her up, but Jake's hands unconsciously tightened on her head, and his mouth was hungry for more.

The hungry tenderness of the kiss surprised Bel into a tremblingly open response. It sent shivers of delight through her body and her self, and her arms came up of their own accord to hold him closer.

She had been thinking long and hard since her talk with Russ. At first of course she wanted to believe that he was right, that Jake just didn't know the state of his own feelings. But as time passed and he never called except for business, she had forced herself to abandon that attractive proposition.

He had told her it was up to her. But that was only if she wanted an uncommitted liaison. She knew very well that if Jake had come to realize he had deeper feelings or more serious intentions, the way Russ said, he would have called her. The number of times she had almost called him...but good sense had won out.

Probably if she weren't a virgin it wouldn't have. But she was so inexperienced, felt so naive. She couldn't bear to call him and find he had lost all interest....

She had missed him almost desperately. But as long as he continued to stay away, Bel figured she could live with that. She dreamed, of course. She imagined him coming to her and sweeping her off her feet, telling her what she wanted to hear.

Sometimes, when the hunger was overwhelming, she didn't imagine him telling her anything at all. In those daydreams he simply made love to her, without a word....

She knew her brother was right about one thing: She was very tired of fighting to keep her virginity. But she hadn't been conscious of the fact until Jake. Maybe she had just worn herself out with too much resistance in the past. She didn't seem to have much now.

If Jake had shown signs of continuing interest...but he hadn't. His voice on the phone, the few times they talked, had been totally impersonal. Friendly, but distant, and hanging up as soon as he could...

So she hadn't prepared any resistance. And now his kiss was melting her, turning her into a vine that wanted nothing more than to wrap herself around him.

The wall intervened. Jake kissed and tasted her lips, but at last the frustration of not being able to press her close made him lift his head.

"Come outside," he breathed. He had noticed a soft-looking bed of grass underneath the weeping willow across the lawn....

Suddenly he came to his senses. He snatched his hands away from her, and swore. "Damn! Sorry, Bel!" He swallowed, feeling like a king-size jerk. Every time he lifted a finger around her, he dug his grave that little bit deeper.

He didn't think he'd ever apologized to a woman for kissing her before. God, that must have been a no-no since the year dot!

It certainly allowed Bel to come to her senses. She took a deep, steadying breath and straightened out of his hold. "Okay, no problem," she said, trying for cool.

They stood there for a moment, neither of them quite panting, but both needing more oxygen than they were getting.

"So, how's everything?" Jake asked at last, gripping the windowsill so as to keep his hands away from her.

"It's all going very well," she said. The quickest way past the embarrassment they both felt was to get down to business. "Have you come to have a look around?"

"That, and to give you some cheques. Mind showing me what's been done so far?"

"I guess we may as well start here." Bel couldn't ever remember feeling so awkward. But Jake just nodded and walked around through the door.

Everything smelled of fresh paint. It looked a whole lot neater than it had the day Brad bought the place. This had been a pottery studio then. Now it looked like a suite of professional offices.

He broke into enthusiastic speech as she showed him the labs and a small kitchenette and washroom. "Well, this is looking just great! You seem to have done a helluva lot of work in a short time."

"With the army Brad hired, it would be a miracle if I hadn't. Want to see the house?"

In silence, she led the way out past the swimming pool and up towards the main house. The sun was high and hot, and the pool looked inviting.

"Is that ready for use?" Jake couldn't help asking.

"Yes, I've been swimming in it for a few days now." Bel paused to flick a switch. The humming stopped. "Hasn't the weather been great?"

That was a nice, safe topic, all right. "How about lunch and a swim?" Jake asked, immediately and uncontrollably moving from safe to high risk. "I know a great seafood place about ten minutes from here."

"Oh, I don't..." Bel hesitated, and Jake suddenly realized where he was headed. The seafood place was where he'd meant to take her when he'd first thought of this and planned the seduction....

"Ah—oh! Just remembered...!"

Bel smiled and her heart calmed down. "Got a date already?"

"Something like that," Jake said, so awkwardly he

knew she must realize it was a lie. What a jerk she must
think he was! What a jerk he *was*.

"Anyway, I've got my lunch in the fridge," she said
firmly, as they crossed the lawn to the back of the house.

He merely nodded and slid open the patio door for her
to enter.

The house wasn't finished yet, of course. Bel had so far
supervised the stripping of old wallpapers and carpets, and
some plastering and construction work. Then the entire
place had been primed with white. Now parts of it, under
the supervision of the interior decorator, were coming to
life.

"It's really starting to look good," Bel said.

She led him up the stairs to the top of the house, where
Brad's office would be. It was a large house, but Brad,
Tallia and the designer had come up with a look that, except for two huge reception rooms that they would use for
formal entertaining, was comfortable rather than elegant.

On the next floor they passed through several rooms
painted entirely in cream. "These aren't being decorated
at the moment—they'll be the kids' rooms eventually,"
Bel told him. "Tallia doesn't want to decorate them till
she knows exactly who for."

Her heart thumped as she glanced around, imagining
Tallia and Brad here, putting up childish wallpaper and
light switches and choosing child-sized furniture. She had
seen her parents do things like that together all her life.

That was what she wanted—the planning and sharing
for the future. With Jake there wasn't any question of future, she knew that, and yet, with him here beside her, she
could imagine it. Not Tallia and Brad, but herself and Jake,
arguing over what was straight and whether there were any
bubbles under the paper, kissing and loving each other in
anticipation of a new birth...

As they went from room to room, Jake began to feel kind of weird. The master bedroom was nearly complete, and he was reminded of his own parents' bedroom, that calm centre of stability in a windy world. Sunday mornings he and his brothers and sisters had congregated for discussions and games and jokes and problem-solving.... No matter how confusing life got, there was always some common-sense light shed on it by his parents on Sunday morning.

Was it homesickness he felt? This funny kind of yearning ache for those moments of utter security? He imagined Tallia and Brad surrounded by the numerous kids they talked of having. How many kids did Bel want?

He himself didn't want any. It wouldn't be fair, because he wouldn't be able to give them anything like the kind of security he'd had, right up to his teenage years. *The worst thing a man like you can do is to have children and then abandon them, the way your grandfather did...promise me you won't do that, Jake.*

But he couldn't quell the image that arose in his mind, of himself in a big bed like this, with a couple of kids leaning over his shoulders as he played one of their games with them.... He remembered his father's helpless attempts to solve a Rubik's Cube, and his own triumph when his father handed it back to him...the look his parents had exchanged when he'd done it inside a minute.

He'd have liked to pass on that kind of self-confidence to a kid. He imagined exchanging that kind of look with...well, for argument's sake, with Bel. It was obvious she would make a good mother.

Pity he couldn't risk it. However good a mother Bel would be, he would never be a good father, in the long run.

The breakup of a marriage destroys a child's self-confidence for years. It wouldn't be fair, Jake.

Bel couldn't stop dreaming as they walked through the rooms. The house was much bigger than anything she would have when she married, probably. But it wasn't the size that attracted her—kids could share bedrooms, after all. She and Tallia had shared a bedroom up until Tallia had left home to try her luck in Vancouver, and mostly it had been great.

It was the *feeling,* as though the house was used to warmth and love and laughter and expected to hold more.

Jake had an easy laugh....

And no doubt plenty of women thought so, Bel reminded herself firmly.

They finished up the tour in the big, old-fashioned family kitchen. A Florida room led off it.

"What is that, a jungle out there?" Jake asked in bemusement.

Bel laughed. "All the plants arrived yesterday, but the decorator isn't back till Monday and I don't know where they all go. It's very pleasant to sit in. I'll be kind of sorry when it's all straightened out."

"Shall we sit out there now?"

"Okay."

Jake belatedly began to wonder where he had left his briefcase. He glanced absently around the kitchen. "I left my briefcase by the pool," he remembered suddenly.

"Well, on second thought we may as well go out there, it's such a fabulous day," Bel said, thinking it would be better not to be inside with Jake for too long.

So they moved back outside, and then Jake said, "You haven't shown me the other outbuilding. What are Brad and Tallia doing with that?"

Bel hesitated. "I think it's going to be the guest house," she said. "Or maybe staff quarters, I don't know."

"Has anything been done on it so far?"

It had been a conscious omission, but really there was no reason not to show him, Bel told herself.

"Yes," she said after a moment. "Come and have a look."

Seven

She led him to the small building that sat at right angles to the labs, and then into the sitting room. "Do you like it? Isn't it a fabulous location? Look at that view!"

The windows of the beautifully sunken sitting room faced west over the sea. Perfect for catching the sunset. On the left, across the wide bay, could be seen the dark firs of Stanley Park, and behind, the skyscrapers of the city. He could see why people would buy out here. The For Sale sign on the house next door flicked briefly on his mental screen.

Not much point, though, unless you planned a family.

"Very nice," he said, looking around approvingly. "A person could live here." He wasn't just saying it. He liked the nice mix of clean lines and full-cushion comfort she seemed to be creating. It was a place that would be cool in the heat of summer and cosy in the rain of winter. "A little different from the house. I like this a lot."

Bel flushed with pleasure. "Tallia asked me to choose the decoration and furnishings. It's a practically unlimited budget and I'm having a really great time doing it."

Jake's eyes widened as he swivelled his head to look at her. "*You* did this? It's terrific."

"Yeah, I'm thinking maybe I should have taken my degree in interior design," she joked. Leading him along the short hall, she opened the door to the bedroom. "There might be more job opportunities."

A big, luscious, king-size bed. Someone had slept in it and forgotten to make it. He stared at thick pillows and sheets swirled with bright hot colours.

They stood in pregnant silence for a moment, while they both wished she hadn't opened this particular door. "It's a very attractive room, Bel," Jake began, and then coughed self-consciously. "Are you living in here?"

"Yeah, I moved down from the big house," she said, and Jake sighed out a kind of pent-up tension. It was fairly obvious only one person had slept in the bed. But of course that wasn't his business.

"It's cosier, since I'm on my own, and anyway, this bedroom is the only one in the whole place that's completely finished." She hastily shut the door and led him to the second room. She hadn't furnished it at all, not knowing whether it should be a second bedroom or an office or a baby's room. She had no idea what Tallia and Brad would do with this place. Leave it empty for guests, probably. But Tallia hadn't said.

They had left his briefcase in the sitting room, and by tacit consent they moved back there. Jake stood for another moment absorbing the environment she was creating.

"It's great, Bel. Can I call you in to decorate my house?" he joked, trying to keep his mind on business.

"Does it need redecoration?"

"Not really. But I've been thinking recently of buying a house out here." Recently was right. Like an hour ago.

Bel's heart gave an uncomfortable kick. "Gosh, what for? What would you *do* out here?"

She meant, he knew, that the life of the city was over an hour's drive away. Showed that she understood his priorities a little too well, maybe.

She was right, though. Jake had no idea why he had imagined that it would be a good idea to buy a house out here in the back of nowhere. So he said, "These places are good investment properties."

"Oh, I see," she said, nodding.

For some reason her tone made him want to recall his words. But what could he say instead? This woman was undermining him in more ways than he cared to think about.

He's thinking of investment, Bel told herself sharply. *Stop daydreaming, girl!*

He sat down and opened his briefcase. "Right, let's get down to business! It's getting late and I'm starving."

"Can I get you something to eat, Jake?" she responded automatically.

Jake paused, then shook his head firmly. "This will only take a few minutes, and then I'll be out of your hair and go grab myself a sandwich somewhere."

So he didn't have a lunch date, whatever else he had on his schedule.

"Oh, but—!" Bel protested. "I may as well make you lunch here."

Jake swallowed. "It would be too much trouble. I can grab something on the way back to Vancouver."

"Do you have to work today? Is that why you're in a hurry?"

"I don't work on weekends anymore," he said, then realized he had just given away an excuse.

Bel lifted her hands shyly, so caught up in the moment she hardly realized what trap she was creating for herself. "Well, then, why not eat here? We don't have to have anything complicated. It won't take any more time than stopping somewhere.'

He didn't *want* to go. "Okay. Thanks, Bel, that would be very nice."

They ate outside, by the pool. Nothing exotic, just some cold sliced ham and a couple of salads and a jar of artichoke hearts with Italian bread to soak up the olive oil, but somehow Jake had the feeling it was all nectar and ambrosia. He didn't think he'd ever had such a delicious meal, which was ridiculous...unless you considered your company.

Bel had never before had the experience of just how much spin romantic excitement could give to ordinary food. She'd had lots of wonderful meals in the best restaurants with men devoted to changing her mind. Some of those men had been pretty difficult to turn down, too.

But Jake was something else again. He was a whole different order of magnitude, as they said in science reports. There was a lazy, hungry admiration in his eyes that she had never seen in a man before, never so desperately wanted to experience. Bread melted on her tongue. The flavour of olive oil was indescribably rich and hauntingly sexual. And as for tomatoes...!

They talked and laughed together about things that neither had ever discussed so deeply with anyone. They experienced the kind of mental closeness that is born out of resisted physical attraction. Each imagined they could enjoy it as a substitute for the closeness of their two hungry bodies.

For an hour they talked, while the physical tension grew to unbearable proportions, and when they could stand it no longer, they changed and swam in the cool water of the pool.

But though they each privately hoped that swimming would take the edge off their hunger and growing need, they were wrong. Jake was a powerful swimmer. He pounded up and down the pool, trying to wear himself out, but he was too aware of her silky seal's body and more leisurely pace beside him in the water.

They passed each other at regular intervals, and then came a moment when they simultaneously arrived at the shallow end and simultaneously stopped for a breather and stood up out of the water.

That was when Bel stared at his powerful, masculine body, wet and glistening in the bright afternoon sun, and felt a wilder mix of lassitude and energy than she could have believed possible. That was when she realized just why she hadn't wanted Jake to leave.

And that was when Jake, his chest heaving with exertion, looked at Bel, with her hair streaming down her back, her wet body sleek and brown as a wild animal's, her beautiful young breasts rising and falling under the snug swimsuit, and realized that he had gone beyond the limits of his control.

That was when he reached for her, pulling her with rough tenderness against his chest, wrapping her with urgent, hungry arms, and, looking into her wide, clear eyes, whispered her name.

And then he bent and kissed her water-beaded mouth, lifted his head and gazed into her eyes again. There was a message there now. She knew he was giving her a last chance to say no. If she did not say it now, there could be no going back.

Held so tightly in his arms, she could not say what she did not mean in her heart.

The silence lasted through several thudding heartbeats, and then Jake bent and lifted her high in his arms and began to climb up the broad wide steps out of the pool.

He carried her to her own bed and laid her down on the sheet, then lay down beside her.

The room was soft with the glow of afternoon sun that, filtered through the trees outside, cascaded through the broad windows.

She still had the air of a wild animal as she looked at him. He had never in his life felt such urgent, compelling desire. His whole being, not merely his sex, trembled with expectation.

Bel had never seen a male body that made her so weak with desire, with need. His chest and arms were so strong, so beautifully, smoothly muscled. The black mat of hair on his chest thrilled her, the power in the shoulders, the slimness of his hips, the obvious strength of his thighs and legs and sex…

His body was both warm and cool to her touch as she ran her hands over his water-beaded skin. His mouth touched hers again, questioning and possessive at the same time, the lips strong but soft as they nibbled gently at hers. Hungry little touches that drove them crazy for more, till he could stand it no more and his lips pressed hers, hard and demanding.

His hands cupped her head, her arms embraced him. He kissed her lips till she gasped, then let his mouth roam over her cheeks, her eyelids, down along her throat, then rolled over on his back and wrapped his arms around her to draw her on top of him.

She fell against his chest and lay there in delight as he smiled up into her eyes. "You make me very very hungry," he said, and his words shivered along her spine, like burning ice. "You're a beautiful wild creature, Bel—so graceful, so sleek.'

He stroked her wet hair that fell down one side of her head in a thick mass, while her heart pounded and her body yearned towards him.

"Jake," she whispered.

His mouth lost its smile, and he drew her head down and his lips searched hers again, more urgently this time, hungrier, seeking with tongue and lips as if for sustenance.

Now his hand left her head and moved down over her shoulder, gripping it hard and pressing her closer while she moaned and melted, then down her back and at last to her hips, her curving haunches.

With sudden hunger he pulled her lower body over, so that she lay directly on top of his sex, and she felt the power of his need for the first time.

She gasped, half in fear, half in drunken, delicious anticipation. Whatever happened after, she could not have said no to this. Not forever. This moment between them had been inevitable from the second she had set eyes on Jake Drummond.

Her body pressed against his with uncontrollable spasms of desire, seeking the release it promised, and he put his hand onto her hip hard, to stop her.

"Stop," he commanded. "It's been a long time, and you are just too much for me."

Words to make her hot and cold, to make her melt and shiver with a deep delight she never dreamed of. No one had ever made her so crazy with need. She hadn't known anything could be like this. He kissed her shoulders, her neck, pulling the wide strap of her suit down over her arm, holding it so that she could draw her arm free of it.

Then he pulled the fabric farther and farther down, kissing the flesh as it was revealed, until her breast was free. The air on her skin was cool, and a moment later the touch of his lips was fire. She moaned, and her hands threaded through his thick hair as his mouth opened over the tender nipple and sent a shock wave of sensation all through her.

He freed her other arm, her other breast, and pushed her up so that they fell free and firm above him.

"Bel, you are unbelievably beautiful," he muttered, as if the words were not practised, but torn from him. His hand slipped up and firmly cupped the curving brown flesh, feeling the weight of it, and he closed his eyes as if the sensation were too strong for him.

Her hand of its own accord slipped to his hip, and then, out of necessity, curved over the hungry hardness of his sex. So strong, so powerful! She smiled, and the breath hissed between her teeth as his lips pressed her nipple again.

"You electrify me," he said. "One sound from you and my body wants to..."

He did not finish, but knocked her hand away from its attempts to pull down the damp fabric of his bathing suit. "Bel, this may not be—" He grabbed for breath and blew it out.

He rolled her over onto her back again, knelt up on the bed and pulled her swimsuit down over her hips and thighs, and then over her ankles.

He looked at her naked body with an expression that electrified her in every cell. "You're way too much for me," he said, squeezing his eyes shut. Her hand reached for his sex again, and he held it away. "I won't last, Bel!"

He pulled her thighs apart and the next thing she knew was a wet heat against her sex that made her shout in wordless surprise. Sensation ricocheted through her so suddenly that her body abruptly arced up against his mouth, and began writhing uncontrollably as heat poured through her system. Heat, and delight of an intensity she had never experienced.

She cried out, and almost wept as a volume of feeling her system did not seem capable of bearing roared and swept through her. She was melting, she was flying, she was fainting, and she wildly cried his name, trying to tell him how good it was.

His control snapped. He struggled out of his trunks and pushed her legs wide while a frenzy of hunger consumed him.

"Bel!" he said hoarsely. "This is unbelievable."

She felt him there, pushing for entry where no one had ever entered, and spread her legs wider to allow him in. Only now did she understand what she had been waiting for all these years. It was for this moment, when for him to enter her was a necessity as strong as the breath in her body. When to have him there would be completion.

She arched her head back into the soft pillow as his hard, insistent sex began to force its way into her virgin flesh. "Oh!" she cried, as the pain of it shivered through the trembling pleasure that coursed along skin and flesh and bones. "Oh, God, Jake, oh, it hurts!"

As he drove home inside her, with a hungrier, more desperate need than he had ever experienced in his life, he heard the wild mix of joy and painful protest, and froze in shocked, stunned surprise as sensation and her cries together told him the truth.

He lifted his head and stared down into her eyes, not believing it.

"Oh, Jake!" she gasped. "Oh, my, I didn't know it would hurt like that! Oh, but don't stop, it's the most wonderful thing I ever..."

His voice was an unrecognizable growl as he hoarsely cried her name. "Bel! Bel, my God, are you a *virgin?*"

She smiled up at him through the tears that had sprung unbidden to her eyes. "Not now," she whispered, and gave him a trusting look that went through him like a knife.

He had never in his life felt such a mix of feeling as what smote him now. Pleasure, fear, hope, delight, anger, passion...the whole spectrum of feeling available to humanity seemed to course through him, flooding his system as if he were a single lamp plugged into a city power grid.

He exploded with a loss of control he had never felt before and hoped he would never feel again. It was birth and death, ten thousand births and deaths, as if he were living every life in his path in one terrible, wild, unbearable second, where pleasure and anguish came together.

He cried her name, and his protest, and his utter, utter ecstasy, arched his back uncontrollably, felt how frail the human system was against such forces, and, far, far too soon, exploded helplessly into her.

Eight

Jake lay on his back beside her, his breathing ragged. Moments passed.

"Why didn't you tell me?" he said at last.

Bel swallowed. A mixture of confusion, disappointment, guilt—she hardly knew what she felt—flooded her. "I—I..."

"You told me you'd had at least two lovers. Why did you lie to me?"

She could no longer remember her motives. "I...I don't know," she faltered.

He swore.

"I didn't know it would make a difference to you," she offered.

"Didn't know it would make a *difference?*" he repeated furiously. He sat up, drawing his legs up, and rested his arms across his knees. He looked sideways down at her, a darkly unreadable expression on his face. "What do you take me for?"

Bel suddenly felt very naked.

"Why does it make a difference?"

"Because you were a virgin and you want commitment and I do not have commitment to offer," he said harshly.

She said nothing, merely sat up and swung her legs over the side of the bed, her back to him. She swallowed. *Love 'em and leave 'em. It's better to concentrate on the love 'em.* But she had had even less than she had imagined in her worst imaginings. *I do not have commitment to offer.*

"Are you so sure about that, Jake?" she asked quietly, though she knew she should not. "No, don't answer, I know you are."

You are not the marrying kind, Jake.

He cursed himself for his stupid, primitive cruelty. And her, for…he had broken a lifelong rule with her, and what could he do about it? Nothing. It was done.

He gave vent to a breath of dry laughter.

"Well, they say there's no such thing as half a virgin, but I guess you come as close as anyone could," he said, in dark self-mockery. "I'm sorry."

It had been a long time, too long, since he…but that wasn't the real reason, and he knew it. It had been making the discovery like that. Jake swung his legs down over the opposite side of the bed, so they sat back to back, the bed between them.

A classic image, he thought cynically.

"It doesn't matter," she said mechanically. She felt so strange, so awkward. So rejected. How was she to know that he had a horror of sleeping with virgins? Most men she knew would have been only too happy to…

"Of course it matters! Dammit, why didn't you warn me?"

It was her turn for a mirthless gust of laughter. "Funnily enough, I almost did, that night at the hotel. But you kept stopping me."

She had a horrible knot at the back of her throat which she knew was tears. She shut her eyes tight. Oh, please let her not cry! Not in front of him!

Bel slipped off the bed and feverishly dragged open a drawer, grabbed a T-shirt dress at random, pulled it over her head. When she surfaced Jake was gone. She went out to the sitting room. Through the window she could see him in his swim trunks, striding over towards the pool changing rooms.

Wondering if he would come back, she took a carton of juice and a couple of glasses from the fridge and set them in the sitting room. His briefcase was still on the sofa, so he had to come back. She didn't know whether she was glad or sorry.

He walked in again a few minutes later, dressed in the casual pants and shirt he had arrived in, but with a look on his face she had never seen there before.

He sat down and accepted a glass from her, holding it between his legs as his elbows rested on his knees.

"Bel, I'm sorry," he said. He shook his head helplessly. "But why the hell—!" He broke off and drank a gulp of the juice, then looked at the glass. "I need something stronger than this," he said. "Have you got any whiskey?"

She shook her head wordlessly. "I think there's some beer up in the fridge in the house."

He pressed the fingers and thumb of one hand to his eyes. "Never mind."

"Jake, I—I knew you weren't the marrying kind when I made my decision. It doesn't matter. It's a choice I made."

He glared at her. "Well, it is not a choice I made!"

"But what *difference* does it make?" she demanded.

"Bel, apart from my first girlfriend when I was seventeen, and we were both pretty ignorant so it seemed fair, I have never, to my knowledge, made love to a virgin. I choose women who know the ropes."

"Why?" she asked forthrightly.

"Because they understand me when I tell them I am not the marrying kind." He paused. "And they have no one to blame but themselves if they try to change my mind and fail."

"Well?"

"Virgins are a particular kind of responsibility."

"I thought your opinion of sex was that its only end was pleasure," Bel pointed out, beginning a slow burn. "How does that change because I'm a virgin?"

The worst thing you can do is take a woman's innocence, Jake.

"Look," he said. "I told you I wouldn't make love with you unless you made it very clear you had changed your mind about demanding some kind of commitment. When you asked me to stay to lunch I knew you still hadn't but, well, we cracked. I cracked. You are extremely sexually attractive and I guess it was a foregone conclusion from the moment we decided I'd stay today. But I cracked, believing you were experienced and that one lapse wasn't going to make all that much difference to your general attitude to casual sex. But this is more than a lapse, isn't it? And I am not going to turn into a husband type overnight."

Anger burned up inside her. How dare he make such assumptions about her wants?

"I don't expect you to change into a husband type overnight!" she exclaimed indignantly. "I made my choice.

I'm sorry I didn't make all the unknowns clear to you in advance, but you had better believe I expected nothing more from you as a result of my choice than the good time you offered.''

"I—"

"What the hell makes you think I'd *want* you for a husband, Jake? That's pretty arrogant, isn't it?''

The injustice of this annoyed him. "You turned me down at the beginning because I wasn't into commitment, Bel. Come on, be fair!''

"*You* be fair! Dammit! I'm entitled to change my mind.''

"And did you?'' he asked in a dead level voice.

She blinked. "Did I what?''

"Did you change your mind, Bel?''

"I—I...''

"When did you decide that it wasn't important to save yourself for a man who, I think I have this right, 'is at least willing to consider that forever might exist'?''

She stared at him, swallowing. "That is none of your business.''

"It never happened, did it? What kind of game were you playing, Bel?'' Jake's eyes were like two black borers drilling holes into her mind. "What exactly did you have in mind?''

"What is *that* supposed to mean?'' she almost shouted.

"I'm beginning to see this from another angle, that's what it means. You knew I wouldn't touch you if I knew you were a virgin. That's why—''

"I *knew?*'' she shouted. "How the hell could I know a thing like that, and what—''

"Come on, your sister's new husband knows all about my personal rules!'' Jake's voice was climbing in volume and intensity. "You never asked Brad about me?''

"No, I never asked Brad about you." She glared at him. "What do you think—I compiled a dossier on you or something?"

"I think maybe you thought you could get to me emotionally if I slept with you and discovered you were a virgin."

Her eyes flashed furious fire. She leapt to her feet and glared down at him. "How dare you? You arrogant—! Get to you emotionally? I don't want to get to you emotionally. A man who's had his mind made up from birth, *in principle,* that he could never be loyal to one woman? Do you think I'm crazy?"

"I think you're a woman—you have lots of company!—who believes in the power of love."

"Listen, Jake, I got your number the first night we met, remember? You took great pains then to let me know what you thought of your best friend falling in love with my sister, how you did your best to prevent it, to *save* him from a fate worse than death. What else did I need to hear, Jake? You weren't my type. *I* am the one, if you remember," she shouted, tapping her own chest with a vigorous finger, "who tried to avoid you. *You* never stopped calling for months! Who was trying to manipulate whom then? Who wouldn't take no for an answer, Jake?"

"If you had told me the truth then, I would have backed off fast enough. For God's sake, stop glowering over me and sit down," he added impatiently, and Bel realized to her embarrassment that she was standing over him, bending to practically shove her face into his. She straightened and flung herself back into her seat.

"My virginity or otherwise was none of your damned business. It still isn't, as far as I'm concerned. What the hell business is it of yours? Then or now!"

"If I'd known I could at least have made sure you would enjoy it!" he said surlily, changing tack suddenly.

"You just told me if you'd known you wouldn't have touched me with a barge pole. Which is it? You can't have it both ways."

He was still talking. "...I treated you like a sexually experienced woman. I didn't take the...a virgin needs more—"

She suddenly understood. He was angry because he felt guilty because the sex hadn't been up to his usual standard. That was all this was. And he now felt an obligation to sleep with her again so that she would enjoy it.

He didn't really want her anymore. But he was trapped by guilt.

Furious hurt struck her a blow so powerful over her heart she nearly blacked out. Her heart went cold, became a dead weight in her breast.

"I enjoyed myself just fine, Jake." she said, in a low, biting voice. "So if that's what's bothering you, you can forget it. You have no responsibility of any kind towards me, now or ever. There is no obligation for a return engagement. I was perfectly satisfied, thank you! Thank you for a lovely introduction to the joys of sex! Now, will you please get out!"

She stood up, her breast heaving.

"Look," he said. "It's not—"

She put up both hands, stopping him cold. "Just go, please!"

He reached for her. "I want to see you again."

Bel jerked back out of his reach. "Well, that's very polite of you, Jake. Yes, thank you, how kind of you to say so! Why don't you give me a call sometime?" she said in a bright, sarcastic voice.

He dropped his hands helplessly. "I will," he said, turning to the door.

"Don't forget your briefcase!"

He wordlessly picked it up. At the door he turned. "I'll call you, Bel."

Her face was stone. She watched him, saying nothing, as he went out and closed the door.

Her anger held her up until she heard his car. Then Bel's legs seemed to fold up of their own accord, and she found she was sitting on the sofa. She stared blindly ahead of her, her eyes stretched wide, trying to think.

She didn't know *what* to think. Was Jake right? Had she done a terrible thing, saddled him with a responsibility of some kind? But why was it a responsibility if *she* didn't consider it one? She had decided to make love with Jake, to take what he had to offer and ask for no more, because she wanted to experience the sexual pleasure he could offer.

She hadn't thought beyond that. She was tired of her virginity, tired of fighting, and why shouldn't she choose an experienced, sexy man like Jake, purely because he excited her? Why shouldn't she have the right...

But it wasn't true. Bel felt the real truth start to flow through her from behind the door in her heart that she had been keeping closed and locked.

She had fallen for Jake. Seriously fallen for him. She had never made any decision. The decision had been made for her when he took her in his arms. Earlier. When she had asked him not to leave.

Bel stood up and began to wander through the rooms, her brain feeling numb. She arrived in the bedroom, where her feet led her, and stood for a moment looking down at the rumpled bed.

Was he right? Had she, in that moment, traded her virginity for a calculated risk? Had she unconsciously hoped that somehow sex would bind him to her?

Or was it simply that she loved him and it was foolish to save herself for some other man? He was the one she wanted, and wasn't half a loaf better than none?

She wasn't even going to get half a loaf. Jake was clearly willing to make good on today's less than ideal outcome, but she was damned if she would let him make love to her out of duty! God, a worse humiliation she could not imagine. She cringed. Her skin crawled just thinking about what that meant.

She was only halfway in love with him. It wasn't desperate yet. If she avoided all contact with him in future…

She looked at the rumpled sheet, at her own bathing suit, knotted and lying on the floor, and remembered the wild physical excitement she had felt, the blissful way he had kissed and touched her, before the piercing pain of…even that had somehow excited her. If he had continued, she would have…

She saw again the surprise on his face, the anguished torment as his pleasure had suddenly erupted…at least she supposed that was what had happened. With so little experience it was hard to be sure. Perhaps his excitement had merely died…no. The shock had broken his control, which he had already told her was fragile.

Maybe that was it. Maybe it was all a question of masculine pride. She was very sure that Jake's sexual confidence stemmed from real talent. Well, he had proved it, in the time before that moment. So he had a reputation to maintain, and he was angry with himself for losing control, and with her for causing it.

But none of that altered the terrible central fact—that he

might feel *responsible* now to see her again, to better his performance record with her.

All his talk about their wild attraction for each other, but it hadn't survived the hurt to his sexual ego.

At last the necessary tears started. Bel flung herself across the bed and howled her bewildered hurt to the walls.

Jake didn't think he'd ever been so angry with another human being in his life. Fury raged in his blood, so that he felt his heart beating in powerful thumps through his whole system.

He was driving with only half his mind on the road, but he didn't even realize it, so furiously was he engaged with Bel in his head. What a mess he had made of that! He hadn't been that clumsy a lover since his first attempts with his first girlfriend, and he sure hoped he would never be so bad a lover again as long as he lived.

And she was a virgin, too. So as well as wrecking her plans to save herself for a committed lover, he had ruined her introduction to lovemaking—him, the great Casanova! Who prided himself on...

But of course, if she hadn't been a virgin, it wouldn't have happened. Jake knew he had been pretty close to the wire with her—right from the moment he kissed her in the pool he had felt that his control was weaker than he had ever felt it. But he had had no serious fears. The problem was, he was more attracted to Bel than he had allowed himself to face. And of course the preceding months of celibacy didn't help.

Finding she was a virgin had wrecked his fragile control at a stroke.

His mind went back to that moment when he had realized that her cry, "It hurts, Jake," was not a response to his size. Women did sometimes react like that to him; it had been a moment before he connected the curious note of surprise in her voice with the difficulties and sensations his body was experiencing. Then it had suddenly been clear.

He had never in his life experienced what he felt then. A mix of emotions and sensations that almost made him black out. Sexual passion like nothing he had known existed seemed to come from nowhere to power through his system and make him completely helpless, as if it had an independent existence and had merely used him as a vehicle.

It had never been like that for him before, not even his first time, fifteen or so years ago.

He had made a complete and total fool of himself. Stroke one and you're out, like the old joke. And pleasure like that—it almost frightened him to remember those seconds when he had had no choice but to surrender to it…something like that could get seriously addictive.

He had never done drugs. The idea of experiencing a physical response that would addict you, take away your self-control, make you something less than human, had always terrified him. He had no interest whatsoever.

What he had experienced in those moments with Bel was a loss of self-control so profound he had seemed to have no self. This both amazed and frightened him.

He realized that it was that feeling that made men propose. During their argument he had suddenly felt the urge to say to her, ''Marry me, Bel,'' and it was that that spooked him worst.

He thought of his grandfather and his own father, marrying when they should have known they weren't capable of sticking to their vows. He had always wondered why they had done it. Now maybe he knew. You could fool yourself, feeling what he had felt with Bel. You could fool yourself into thinking you had found the woman who would keep you interested all the rest of your life.

But neither of them had succeeded in doing that. His grandfather had cheated on both his wives, and made his first wife so deeply bitter she never married again. His father—well, his mother had always put up a terrific show of being happy, but he knew from his grandmother that his father cheated regularly and made her life emotional hell.

He remembered overhearing an argument about it, a long time ago. He had come home unexpectedly one Saturday afternoon when hockey practice had been cancelled. He had come in the front door, very unusually, because his friend's father had dropped him off at the curb instead of in the driveway and his gear was clumsy and heavy.

His parents were in the kitchen, deep in an argument more bitter than any of their normal little fights that flared up regularly and almost always ended in laughter. Jake hadn't meant to eavesdrop. He had just been frozen to the spot by the sound of deep, wrenching hurt in his mother's voice, the guilt in his father's.

Only for a minute, but long enough to understand what had happened. He had immediately turned and gone out again, walking around to Brad's and hanging out with him till he was late for dinner.

By then his parents had discovered his hockey gear by the front door. They questioned him closely about when he had left it there, whether he had been inside.

He lied. He said he'd just dumped it and then gone with Neil and his dad...and he pretended not to notice their relief.

So he'd known from the age of fifteen that what his grandmother said about him was true. His father was a chip off the old block, and he was another of the same.

He thought of hearing that hurt in Bel's voice one day because of something he had done, because he had broken faith and his vows, and maybe with their child in the next room overhearing—that was one of the ugliest scenes he could imagine in an ordinary life. He would never do that to a woman—he would never do it to Bel.

Nine

"Hi, Mom."

"Annabel! Is that you?"

"Yeah, it's me. Were you thinking it might be Tal?" Most people, even family members, had trouble distinguishing the two sisters' voices.

"Not really. They called a day or two ago. They really seem to be having a wonderful time in all those exotic places."

"Yeah, I talked to Tal a while back when they were in Hawaii. Sounds fabulous, doesn't it?"

Mother and daughter chatted about the honeymoon couple for a few minutes before Bel asked casually, "What are you all up to this weekend? Can I come home for a visit?"

She had waited and wondered and hoped that Jake would call and then been glad when he didn't, and then started hoping again…for almost two weeks. She couldn't stand another weekend of it. Not all by herself. It didn't help, either, that her days were no longer filled with studying, and that most of her university friends had disappeared into new lives or taken the summer to travel. When Bel felt desperately alone and yearning, she told herself firmly that it wasn't really Jake she was missing, but her old life. Sometimes she believed it.

"Yes, we'll be here. I'm not so sure about the boys, but your father and I will be. When will you come—Friday night?" her mother asked, and then added immediately, "Don't come Friday night, darling, the traffic is so awful out of the city and I always worry about you. Can you come in the early afternoon?"

"I wish I could. I can't get it together at all for Friday, Mom. This place is going to be full of painters and decorators and I have to be here all day. And that means there are a few things I'll have to wait to do on Saturday. Is that okay?"

"We'll see you sometime Saturday, then. Your dad will probably be barbecuing dinner, so don't be *too* late, okay? You know how he likes an appreciative audience."

Bel laughed, and although she had felt perfectly calm until the second before, for some reason her breath caught on a sob.

"Bel, you're crying! What is it? What's the matter?"

She dashed a hand over her eyes. She was far too quick to burst into tears these days. Oh, if only he would call! Even on business. If only she could hear his voice…

"Oh, nothing, really. I was just wondering suddenly when I'm going to meet a guy like Daddy." She sniffed. "If ever."

She could feel a real bout of tears threatening. Oh, God, why had she done it? Why had she asked him to stay for lunch? She had known it was dangerous! Why had she let him kiss her....

Her mother wasn't fooled. "Bel, are you sure this will keep till Saturday? Maybe you should come home tonight."

"I can't, Mom, I told you, there are so many men coming tomorrow.... It's all right, it'll keep."

The deep loving concern in her mother's voice was making it harder to control her tears. Why did she have to fall in love with a man like Jake, a man incapable of love, instead of someone like her father, someone she could have a lifetime of love and working together with? What was wrong with her that she was in love with a Casanova?

"Has something happened, Bel? I mean, obviously it has, but—have you been hurt or anything? Because if so, I can..."

"No, nothing like that, Mom," she assured her mother hastily, fighting not to let her face crumple completely, squeezing her eyes tight, pressing her lips together. "Just a little of what you'd call—man trouble, I guess. I'll tell you Saturday."

Her mother was silent. "I'm coming down."

"Mom, I'm fine. Please don't come," Bel said desperately. She couldn't bear to talk about it here, with her mother sitting on the sofa where Jake had sat.... She wanted to be safe. "Please, I'd rather come home."

Her mother paused. "Are you sure, Bel?" And when Bel assured her that it was what she wanted, she insisted, "But will you call me tomorrow? I can never get hold of you, you always seem to be on some other part of the estate. Just how big is that place Brad bought, anyway?"

Her mother always had the knack of turning tears to laughter. A watery chuckle escaped Bel. "I'm not sure in terms of acreage. A football field or three."

"Bel, is it—is it Brad's friend Jake who's causing the man trouble?" her mother asked gently.

She squeezed her eyes tight against the flood that threatened. "Right first time, Mom!" she said, mock cheerfully, then sniffed.

She could hear her mother expel an unhappy breath. "Oh, dear!"

"Yeah," Bel agreed. "See you Saturday."

"I'll clear the decks for Saturday night. Your father and the boys can maybe go to a movie after the barbecue. Okay?"

It was all so natural, so normal. She had always imagined having a marriage just like her parents', raising kids and making them feel just as loved as she had always felt....

Under her hand the phone rang, and thinking it was her mother again, Bel lifted it on the first ring.

"Hi, Bel. It's Jake."

She gripped the receiver tightly, her back stiffening with the animal recognition of danger, and pressed her lips together. Of course, she had known he would have to call sometime, but she had been hoping to be in control of herself when he did.

"Oh, Jake!" She swallowed convulsively. "Hi."

"How's, uh…how's it all going?"

Her heart was suffocating her. "Fine," she said gruffly. Then, "One or two hitches, but they all got sorted out."

"Sorry I didn't check in with you more regularly, but you—you can always call me, you know."

Bel took a deep, trembling breath. "Yeah, I know. I didn't need help. It was okay, Jake."

"Can I see you for dinner, Bel?"

Her heart gave one horrible jolt, and nearly knocked her

off her feet. Carefully Bel looked around for the sofa and sank down into it.

She had prepared for such a moment with a hundred different responses, but when day after day had passed and it had not come, she had forgotten her definitive reply.

She thought of her conversation with her mother, thought of her mother and father, and how happy they were, how she had always hoped to find a man capable of devotion like her father's.

Whatever he wanted from her, what did Jake have to offer her but heartache? It had taken him almost two weeks to call. Two weeks to make up his mind that he could be bothered seeing her.

What could that mean for her but future grief?

"I'm sorry, Jake, I'm busy."

He was angry—with himself, with life, with everything. He had nearly killed himself trying not to make this call. The obvious lie now made him furious. It was as if a wildcat were clawing at his guts.

"When?" he demanded.

"Wh—what?"

"I haven't mentioned a night, Bel," he pointed out dryly.

Bel opened her mouth silently, trying to get the air she needed without him hearing. Trying not to sob aloud. Her nerves were so tight they must be constricting the blood supply to her brain. She felt faint.

"Oh! I thought—I assumed you meant tonight!" she faltered.

"In that case, how about tomorrow night?"

She couldn't lie about being busy forever. He would chase her down like a fox, only she had no lair. It would be better to face things. "No thanks, Jake," she said.

"Why not?"

"I don't want to see you."

"I want to see you."

She opened her mouth again in a soundless cry as the words hit her. He spoke with a low, intense hunger she could hardly bear to hear.

She tried to swallow, but her mouth was too dry. "No," she said finally.

"Bel, please."

His voice was raw with need. Bel began to shake. "Jake...be fair," she pleaded.

He had been fair all his life. He had backed off any woman he thought emotionally vulnerable. He had tried to do the same with Bel, and found the old incantations no longer worked. He wanted to see her. To hell with being fair.

"All's fair in—" he began, then realized what word came next and choked.

Silence. *Don't you ever tell a woman you love her, Jake. That's not playing fair.*

"Is it?" she said sadly. So it wasn't what she wished for, the need she heard. He hadn't gone away and discovered he had a heart, or anything like that. He couldn't even say the word.

"We have to get together anyway. What about the work on the house?" Never in his life had he so mishandled a woman. Jake clenched his teeth on a silent curse. Maybe he should go and take a refresher course at the university of life.

"I told you, the work on the house is going fine."

"Why won't you see me?" he pleaded. Had some woman in the past said that to him? Had he at all understood what had motivated her? Jake wondered, hearing a distant echo as the words spilled awkwardly from him. Probably more than one. And the answer had been, even if he hadn't expressed it that way—because you are starting to think long-term, and in the end you will get hurt.

He had wanted to save them pain. Only now did he realize that he had maybe not saved them pain—just made them face it sooner rather than later. Maybe he should have let them make the choice.

"Because a one-night stand is a one-night stand, and I think we should leave it that way," Bel said.

Yes, he had used words something like that. Not "one-night stand," precisely; he had never been big on one-night stands. But the sentiment was pretty much the same. No commitment.

And he knew damned well that in her mouth it was a lie. She had never thought in terms of a one-night stand. No woman who had managed to hold on to her virginity to the age of twenty-two willingly gave it up for a one-night stand.

But he had given her such a lousy introduction to sex maybe she couldn't…he didn't want to think about that. If she would see him, he could correct that first impression, he knew that. He could make good on that, at the very least. For her sake.

"Look, if you…Bel, it gets better," he pleaded. "I can—we can—I'm sorry I spoiled it, but believe me when I tell you it can only get better."

Unless, of course, she was now physically repelled by him. But he wouldn't think that. He would go crazy if he thought that. He didn't understand why. Pride, maybe. But right now he didn't feel as though he had any pride left. Hell, he was practically begging.

Bel closed her eyes, squeezing the hot tears tight. She covered the receiver so that he wouldn't hear as she sniffed and swallowed, stifling her feelings. Who would have thought any man would take so much pride in his love-

making abilities that he would insist on a replay when—
oh, God, and she felt so weak! If he went on insisting, she
would cave in, and then where would she be?

The fact was, although Jake obviously despised himself
for his sexual performance, she had never been so thrilled
by a man's touch. Of course she had been sorry when it
was over so quickly; she had wanted it to go on...but in
the minutes leading up to that moment of disappointment
she had felt something she had never experienced with
either Nat or Will. She had remained a virgin in spite of
some very intense necking then...but she could never have
called a halt with Jake. She had been wild for completion
practically from the moment he kissed her.

If he considered it so humiliatingly bad a performance,
what would the real thing do to her?

She could guess: it would bind her to him like a sailor
in a storm who lashes herself to the mast, hoping to escape
with her life.

But the mast never cut the ropes that bound the sailor.
Jake would, one day soon or late, ruthlessly cut the ties
that she felt already wrapping her to him. And then she
would drown in the stormy sea. Drown? She would bleed
to death. Because the bonds would carry her lifeblood.

She wanted to make love with him again. Wanted it with
a force that felt like deep-seated, lifelong need.

But she wasn't going to make love with him again. She
was not going to sail deliberately into a deadly storm. She
was going to turn around and head for home before the
wind got too high.

"Please believe that, Bel."

When Jake heard what he had just said, he almost
groaned aloud. He sounded like a twenty-year-old dweeb.
What the hell was the matter with him? Why didn't he just

use his charm on her, flirt with her, build a little sexual anticipation into the conversation, dammit?

Because he couldn't. Every skill had deserted him. For some reason around Bel he had been clumsy from the very beginning. He had broken nearly every rule in the book right from day one.

Including his own prime directive: *Do not interfere with virgins.* He should have guessed that about her, he really should, but he had lost his grip. He did not know why. All he knew was that he kept tripping over his own feet. He felt like a fool. He wanted to forget her. He wanted to walk away from the scene of the disaster. *She* wanted him to walk away from the scene of the disaster.

He had never, not once in fifteen years, pushed himself on a woman who had expressed reluctance. Flirtatious reluctance was a different thing—of course he had pursued women who weren't sure, or who had refused because they wanted to be pursued.

But when a woman didn't seem to like him, to invite him…he always, but always backed off. But dammit, she had been a virgin, and he had a responsibility…

Was that what drove him, in the final analysis? He couldn't be sure. He hoped so.

"Jake, this is your pride talking," she said, as if picking up on that thought. "And I've already told you not to…that you don't have to worry about that. Now, please. I don't want to see you."

"I have to give you your paycheque," he said abruptly.

This stopped her. She did need the money. Her university loan payment was due next week, unless she wanted to go and argue with the bank for a delay.

"Mail it to me," she said at last.

"It'll take ten days to get there," he reminded her. "I know damned well you need the money."

She had mentioned her university loan that day by the pool, told him she had deliberately undertaken repayment immediately. He had advised her to wait till she had her life a bit more settled, had a permanent job, but she hated being in debt. And of course she was optimistic about finding a real job soon.

So he had a stick, or a carrot, he wasn't sure which. And he couldn't stop himself using it. He had never been so grateful for lousy city delivery.

"I don't need it right away," she lied. It meant borrowing from her parents, Bel knew, and she had sworn to herself she would ask them for no more money once her exams were over. But if the alternative was… "Send it by courier," she said, instantly demolishing her own lie.

"Bel, I promise—" he began, and with a surge of panic she could feel her determination begin to waver.

"No."

"I have to see you," he said, with an urgency that equally thrilled and terrified her.

"Why?" she demanded, goaded.

This seemed to stop him. "Because I—you—"

"Have you changed your mind about anything, Jake?" she asked, her voice hard to prevent emotion showing through.

"Bel, I—"

"Have you?"

She listened and heard nothing but silence. Bel's heart twisted in pain, and she squeezed her eyes tight shut. She must learn to stop hoping. No doubt she would, in time. Just now, with every heartbeat, she hoped again. If he said no ten times running, she would still hope that his eleventh answer was, I have changed, I love you and can be a loyal partner….

"Jake, I am not a scientific experiment, you know. I'm

sorry for your bruised pride, but I think you should just accept that with one woman you did not perform to your usual standard and leave me alone. What you're doing isn't right.''

Silence again. Then he said softly, and as if it cost him an effort, ''All right, Bel. Sorry.''

Bel squeezed her eyes shut, pressed her lips together, and tried to breathe silently as the hurt of her success at getting what she didn't really want pierced her. Then, without another word, she gently set the receiver back in the cradle. She knew she couldn't trust herself to speak again.

If she had, she might have told him it didn't matter, that she would see him on whatever terms he cared to name.

Ten

Friday was exhausting. It didn't help that she had spent most of last night after Jake's phone call awake. Bel wandered around the house in a daze, watching and talking to men and women who were laying carpet, installing natural wood floors, putting the finishing touches on the fireplace, the kitchen or the paintwork, installing a stained glass window beside the front door and hanging chandeliers.

She was glad to have so much to occupy her, glad to have no time to think, because she might have thought about Jake, and if she thought about him her resolution might weaken.

Over and over she heard his voice in her mind. *I have to see you.* Oh, if only that meant what she wanted it to mean. Why shouldn't he change? Why shouldn't she be the one to break through his defences? He had said they had something special....

But he had been talking about physical reactions, another part of her reminded her ruthlessly. And it was stupid to dream of breaking through his defences, when it was likely that he didn't *have* defences and instead—just didn't have the capacity to love deeply.

But still a yearning voice urged her to call him. Another voice told her she was lucky to get out when she did. She felt like a battlefield where two different selves wrestled for control of her behaviour.

By six o'clock everyone had left except the interior decorator's assistant, who was retaking all measurements.

"If you want to go, I have a set of keys," he said. "You don't have to hang around for me."

Bel sighed gratefully. "Thanks, Michael. I'm dying for a cool soak in the tub."

But as she lay in the beautiful shell-shaped ivory porcelain bath she herself had chosen, relaxing as the dust and fatigue of the day floated away, she saw the long, empty evening stretching ahead of her and her heart beat anxiously. She could not bear another night of thinking about Jake. She would have to do something, call somebody, or maybe defy her mother's advice and drive home tonight.

A book wouldn't do tonight. Television or a movie would be no help. What was playing on the screen of her own mind was far too vivid to be drowned by such faint external stimuli.

What she needed was company. But she didn't want *company*. She wanted Jake. It was one thing to run home to her family; it was another thing, she had discovered during these past two weeks, to call up a friend and then spend the whole evening either blabbing her sorrows, or staring vacantly into space hearing nothing of what her friend said.

There was no real solution. She knew that. She just had to get through it. It was going to be a day-by-day thing, and today was just another day. It was like being sick. You just had to suffer and believe that, however it felt now, one day you would be well again.

It would stop hurting. One day, it would stop hurting. One day she would think of Jake and be touched by nothing but the faint memory of a bad time she had been through. She might not even remember his face.

One day.

She got out of the tub and slipped into the shower to rinse off. Then she towelled herself briskly, and told herself she was feeling much better. In the bedroom she put on a pair of worn green combat jeans and a cream top, just in case she decided on a movie after all. Or maybe she *would* call up a friend for a quick pizza. She combed her hair and with a long clasp comb fixed it back into a tail, then made up her eyes.

This was what she needed, the performance of routine tasks…maybe she should do the vacuuming or something.

But she made no move to do the vacuuming. Instead, she wandered to the kitchen and stared vacantly into the fridge, wondering if she was hungry enough to eat. Just as absently she closed the fridge door again. She wandered down the steps into the sitting room and gazed out the broad window past the green trees to the sea.

An hour at least till sunset. The lowering sun sparkled on the water, but the trees were tossing in the wind, and she could see rain clouds gathering in the south. She stood there gazing out, half hypnotized, empty of thought.

She was waiting, but she did not know for what. Not for Jake. She was waiting for something that would never come from Jake—she was waiting for love.

When the knock sounded on the door, though, she thought only of the interior designer's assistant. Probably he didn't have the keys after all, or he had forgotten to tell her something—that was all that was in her mind as she stepped to the door and flung it defencelessly wide.

Her heart gave a tortured twist and stopped beating, her mouth fell helplessly open, her skin rushed with icy shivers.

"Jake!" she breathed.

He was tall, dark, strong, filling the doorway squarely as if to prevent her escaping to freedom past him. But she made no move. She froze where she was, staring at him, her eyes stretched wide.

"I want to talk to you," he said. He came in, putting one hand on her arm to guide her back, took the door from her grasp and closed it.

She had been able to say no on the phone, but she was helpless in his physical presence. Helpless with longing. When he reached for her she lifted her arms up around his neck, and Jake responded with a hold that nearly drove all the breath from her body. He bent his head over her invitingly lifted face and his mouth crushed hers with desperate, hungry ardour.

She melted against him with a little sob.

His upper body fell back against the door and she was plastered all along the length of him, crying and laughing with the desperate relief of seeing him. His hand came up to cup her head, and he alternately tasted and devoured her lips with wild passionate kisses.

Then suddenly his arms released her, his lips abandoned hers. She felt his hands grip her arms, and he straightened and set her away from him. He breathed heavily for a moment, then took her hand in a firm grip.

"We have to talk," he said.

He led her into the sitting room, down the steps into the well, and made her sit on a sofa. On either side of the empty stone fireplace broad window panels gave onto the sea and the wind-tossed trees. Even though the sun still shone golden, the first drops of rain were speckling the glass.

He stood looking at her. As if in a dream, she couldn't breathe. He looked grave, so grave she knew he could not be going to say what she wanted to hear. But his eyes swept so hungrily over her face that still she couldn't prevent the little tendrils of hope from slipping up to wrap her heart, making it beat with tremulous excitement that nearly choked her.

"How have you been, Bel?" he asked carefully, looking at her. Not a casual question.

"Fine!" she lied brightly.

He nodded as if that was no more than he had feared. "Well, I haven't been fine," he said roughly. "I've been living through hell."

She tried to swallow and couldn't. She tried to speak and couldn't. She licked her dry lips while the silence went on, and finally managed words.

"What is it you're saying, Jake?"

"You said once, there was no chance for compromise between two positions as far apart as ours. I agreed with you then. Now I'd like to find out if that's really true. If there's no way we could—agree about some things and disagree about others. Find a compromise."

"Why?" she asked, staring down at her hands in her lap.

"Because I am going out of my mind without you."

Her heart kicked painfully.

"But you still can't—can't think of giving up other women for me?" she suggested softly. "Are you here to ask me to buy a share of Jake Drummond for a while?"

He closed his eyes and she saw that she had hurt him.

"Bel, it isn't like that," he said. "It's not that I—want

anyone else. It's not that I even feel, right now, that I ever will. I don't. Right now I feel as if I love you so desperately I could never lay a finger on any other woman no matter what happened between you and me.''

''Oh, God, Jake!'' she pleaded, squeezing her eyes tight to prevent tears. ''Oh, Jake, don't say that if it isn't true!''

''It isn't true, Bel.'' She gasped and opened her eyes to gaze at him.

''I know myself better than that. I know what line I come from. My father and my grandfather—they both...'' He paused and took a deep, rasping breath. ''Bel, they both made the lives of the women they loved misery. They both cheated...my grandmother was embittered all her life. She never married again after my grandfather divorced her for another woman. My mother—I don't know how my mother copes with it.''

She was crying before he finished, hot tears burning down her cheeks. He sank to the sofa beside her and took her hand in his. Just the sight of that hand, those strong but graceful fingers grasping hers so tightly, made her shake.

''Bel, I never want to do that to you. I never want to make promises to you and then break them and hear that tone in your voice that I heard in my mother's, or see you look at the world with eyes like my grandmother's, and know that I have been the one to do that to you.''

She took her hand out of his and pressed both hands to her face. She sobbed loudly once. ''Oh, Jake, are you sure about this? Maybe you could be different if you made up your mind....''

He shook his head. ''Maybe I could, Bel, and maybe it would be just blind, groundless hope talking. Nearly fifty percent of marriages end in divorce—that's how one of my partners earns his entire living. And I'd be starting out with two strikes against me.''

There was silence. She wiped her cheeks, sniffed, swallowed, and sat up a little straighter.

''What were you going to suggest?''

''If you are happy without me, nothing. You asked me not to call you, but I thought—maybe it would be truer to say I hoped—that this is harder on you than you want to admit.''

She thought of her days and nights of wandering misery, of the ache of longing. Had he felt that way? If he did—

''No, I haven't been happy, Jake,'' she whispered simply. ''I love you. I've never loved anyone like this. It hurts so much. But I don't see—''

She glanced up in time to see his eyes close helplessly, felt the effort it cost for him to draw breath, and the words died.

''Oh, God, Bel, I didn't—I was hoping it hadn't gone so deep with you—no, what a lie that is!'' He turned and faced her, grasping her arms above the elbows, then releasing them to cup her head. He kissed her tenderly, his passionate yearning held in check but making his hands tremble against her hair.

His lips were as hungry, as tender, as loving as anything she had ever dreamed of. He lifted his mouth and rested his forehead against hers.

''I love you, Bel, and I wish I were the kind of man you need and want, but I can't be sorry that you love me. I wish anything were different except that. I can't wish away your loving me.''

Her heart was shaken to its roots. The tears flooded her eyes and spilled over. He bent and kissed them from her lips and cheek, and her heart trembled unbearably with every caress.

He lifted his head, and looked into her eyes. She asked carefully, ''What do you want, Jake? I guess you—don't want to get married.''

His hand found one of hers, lifted it and brought it to his mouth. He kissed first the back, then turned it over and buried his mouth in her palm. She felt the damp of his own tears on his cheek.

''Bel,'' he said hoarsely. She had never heard a voice so tortured, and wondered if that was how it would sound when he was confessing to her that he had found someone else. Or would he speak coolly, having lost all feeling for her?

''No, it's all right, Jake. Just tell me what you—'' Her breath caught uncontrollably in her throat. ''Just tell me what you want.''

''I can't say—let's get married,'' he said. ''I can't make a vow like that knowing what I know about myself.''

Her heart seemed to curl up against the pain. ''Do you—will you ever want children?''

There was silence while he held her hand and gazed down at it.

''I see,'' she whispered. ''What, then, Jake?''

''I want to see you. I want to love you. I want to live with you.''

''For how long?'' she asked, bewildered.

''Bel, I—''

''For as long as it lasts?'' she interrupted.

''Yes—no!'' He took her head between his hands again and gazed at her. ''Don't you see that I don't know anything? I can't answer you because I don't know.''

She drew out of his hold. ''Funny, you never struck me as a coward, Jake.''

He let his hands fall. ''Am I a coward?''

''I met your brothers and sisters at the wedding. And

your parents. They seem happy. I guess she's told you some things about it, but has your mother ever said that she wishes she hadn't married your father?''

"She used to tell my grandmother about it. She and my grandmother had that in common. Mom never let us kids suspect. But I—''

"You said…you talked about hearing hurt in her voice. When did you hear that?''

"I came home early one afternoon when a hockey practice got cancelled. I heard them in the kitchen arguing about it. Up until then I always thought they were really happy. I went to Brad's, and when I got home again my mother was her usual self. That's when I figured it was all a front. If she was like that after what I'd heard—I asked my grandmother about it, and she said, 'If she is going to keep him for the sake of you children, of course she has to put a brave face on it.'''

"What a horrible thing to say!'' Bel exclaimed indignantly. "How old were you?''

"Fifteen.''

"No wonder you got such a cynical view of marriage! What gave her the right to tell you why your mother stayed with your father? That's—''

"I guess she felt that a lifetime of loneliness gave her the right. She was trying to warn me against myself, let me see how the pain I caused wouldn't just end because I walked away, or because my wife forgave me.''

She stared at him. "Is your grandmother still alive?''

"No. You'd have liked her, I think.''

"*Liked* her? I'd have liked to give her a good punch in the head! Talking to a fifteen-year-old like that! A thing like that could destroy a kid's confidence completely.''

He didn't tell her how much earlier it had started. "But

if it's true, Bel, isn't it better that I got a little self-knowledge, even at that price?''

''My mother says nobody ever learns self-knowledge through being told by somebody else, so if that's what she wanted, which I doubt, her efforts were wasted.''

''Anyway, it didn't affect my confidence. I never—''

''Oh, you're just terrified of marriage as part of the natural condition?''

''I'm not terrified of marriage.''

She looked at him in astonishment. ''What else do you call it, Jake?''

''A rational understanding that my genetic background makes me and marriage incompatible.''

. She could almost have laughed. She stared at him, but he really did believe what he was saying.

''Genetics isn't everything. You were raised in a loving home, even if there was a problem between your parents, weren't you? That kind of home life counts for something.''

He looked down at her. ''Are you asking me to marry you, Bel, and have kids, in spite of what I know about myself? Could you put up with finding lipstick on a shirt one day, or a woman's phone number in my pocket? With calling me at the office late at night and finding I'm not there after all?''

She was silent. ''Is that the way it would be?''

''I don't know! Don't you see that until I met you I never understood that my father and grandfather fell in love and married believing it would last? I never expected to love anyone deeply. I thought they married feeling no more for their wives than the kind of affection I felt for the women I dated. I believed that was all there was, at least for men like us. I thought it had to do with the times they lived in, that they married because that was what society expected of them. I swore I would never do that.''

He paused.

''I never expected to have trouble with my decision. I knew I'd miss having kids, but when I thought of what my grandmother said about how children suffer, how my own father had suffered—well, it wasn't so hard.

''But I had no idea love was like this, did this to a man. I see now that my grandfather must have felt like this—but still he could cheat on the woman he loved. It feels impossible to me, yet don't I have to accept it? I don't know myself, how can I know the future?''

''So you just want me to live with you, no promises, is that it?''

''That's what I'm asking.''

''No marriage, no children. I just live with you until your passion has died and then when you start to cheat uncontrollably I can go off and find myself a man who's better husband material, and if I'm still young enough I can have children with him?''

He winced at this painting of the picture, but she was right. He could hear the hurt in her voice. It seemed that he was doomed to make a woman unhappy whatever he did.

''Bel,'' he pleaded softly. ''Bel.''

''You said compromise, Jake. But it seems to me that what you mean is, I compromise. I give up my dreams of a committed relationship, of stability and permanence and loyalty and a family—all for love. What do you give up, Jake? Some house room?''

''Bel, I—what do you want?'' he demanded harshly, goaded beyond his endurance. ''Do you want to marry me, knowing the risks? Do you want to have kids and run the risk that one day one of us will be bringing them up alone with the other visiting at weekends to take them to a movie? Or that we'll stay together and you'll hate me for what I've done and what I am? Shall we get married in spite of everything I've told you?''

He lifted his head and stared at her, his eyes dark and tormented.

''I'll do it, Bel. I'll marry you if that's what you say you want.''

Eleven

She sat gazing into his eyes. She seemed, in this moment, to see straight into his soul, and what she saw there was everything that would make him the right husband for her. She saw honesty, decency, a determination to do right, intelligence, passion, deep love…and a man who had been taught to doubt and despise himself for being a man.

She felt her whole life was waiting with bated breath for her decision. What she chose now would colour every day and night of her life until she drew her last breath.

Slowly, she sat back. Slowly, reluctantly, she shook her head.

''No, Jake, that's not what I want,'' she said, gentle but determined.

He closed his eyes and she knew he had been hoping that she would say yes.

''I can't take the responsibility for who you are, Jake. Remember when you said to me that if I wanted you I couldn't just tempt you and expect you to make the running?''

"What's it got to do with this?"

"You're asking me to bear the responsibility for your decision. We'll get married, but if you're weak, well, I knew that was a risk when I married you."

"I can't pretend I don't know what I know, Bel."

"No, I know."

"What do you want from me?"

She shook her head, feeling as though she wanted to take back every word she had spoken, wanted to say *marry me at any cost*. But she couldn't. A part of her knew more than she knew herself, knew that she was asking for misery if she took him on such terms.

"I don't know, Jake. Maybe nothing. All I know is, I can't take the responsibility for your decision. And I won't live with you on the terms you offer. It would be just postponing the misery."

He swallowed and she heard him curse helplessly under his breath. "What then, Bel?" he asked in a choked voice. "What are we going to do? Date from time to time till you find a man who—has more to offer you?"

"I can't think about it anymore right now," she protested. Feeling was so thick in her throat and stomach that it felt like an ocean of tears. "I don't know."

"Bel, you can't say you won't see me at all."

"Can't I?" she asked, as if she really didn't know. She lowered her head and shut her eyes, putting a hand over her mouth. She breathed carefully, trying not to let feeling push past the knot in her throat. "Maybe you're right, maybe I can't. I don't know, I have to think." She looked up at him. "Please go, Jake. I can't think with you here."

A gust of wind hit the house, driving rain against the windows with a wild smash. Outside, trees tossed and danced in the wild wind. The sky was nearly black with sunset and storm.

Jake closed his eyes, nodded, and opened them again.

"All right, Bel," he said. "All right." Then he reached for her, wrapped her in his arms and held her, pressing his face against her hair. "Bel," he whispered helplessly.

"Jake!" she cried, and her control melted away and sobs pushed up from her throat. "I don't see how you can give in like that! Why can't you just make up your mind you won't be like him?"

Don't you ever make a woman cry the way I've cried.

"Don't cry, Bel," he begged. "I'm sorry. I'm sorry."

She choked back her grief and looked at him. He stroked the hair from her face with such tenderness another sob escaped from her throat.

"I shouldn't have told you. I should have pretended I didn't love you and walked away. I'm sorry."

She began to weep softly, and he drew her against his chest and held her there, cradling her head with a loving protection that made her feel she would be safe with him forever.

The contradiction between what she felt and what he had told her made her weep even more. But at last her sobs subsided and she drew away from him, leaning forward to pull some tissues out of the little box on the table. She wiped her face, blew her nose, and smiled at him.

His own face was wet. They gazed at each other like soldiers who have been through a terrible battle, and are not sure yet whether they have sustained a life-threatening injury.

Then Jake drew her into his arms and gently lowered his lips to hers.

Sweetness pierced them as their lips met, a solace for the pain they had inflicted on each other. They drew closer together, and she sank against his chest, seeking the comfort that could come only from him, as though he were her safe refuge from the pain that he himself had caused.

Outside, the storm moved directly overhead, sending wind and rain pounding against the house in huge gusts.

His control shivered and broke as he drew her closer and closer to his heart. He kissed her mouth, and lifted his head. "Let me love you, Bel," he whispered. "Let me love you."

A gulf opened within her, the raw hunger of the soul, and she moaned and murmured her yearning as his mouth was alternately tender and fierce with hers.

He guided her down onto her back on the sofa, still in his arms, and followed her down, lying over her, cradling her against his chest. He stroked her face, looking into her eyes, and murmured her name, then bent again to trace her lips with his own.

"You are so beautiful," he said hoarsely. He reached behind her head to undo the clasp that held her hair, and tossed it aside as her hair spilled free. He lifted a curl to his mouth. "So beautiful."

His hand trembled with possessive tenderness as he traced the line of her forehead, eyebrow, her cheek, her ear, her lips. "I've been like a crazy man without you."

Everywhere he touched her, her flesh ached and sang with bittersweet yearning. She felt as though she had come home, as though in Jake's arms was where she belonged. She was a fool if she thought she was only half in love with him. She was in love with him as deep as being went. She cleaved to him, body and soul.

"No, Jake," she whispered.

"Bel!" His voice was urgent with need.

"Jake, no."

"Bel, I want to love you," he whispered hoarsely. "Let me love you."

She struggled, and as if it required a harder battle with himself than he had ever fought before, he lifted himself away from her and let her sit up.

"Jake, I can't make a decision like this now," Bel said in a low voice. "I have to think."

"Bel, whatever you decide, let me love you now. Let me show you how good it can be."

She shook her head. "I think I'd rather not know."

He went still. He said, in a voice kept firmly level, "That sounds as if you've already made up your mind."

"I don't know," she said again. Her heart was torn from its moorings and lashed in rhythm with the wind that shook the house.

He stood. She looked up at him, saw his white face, his dark eyes, and almost lifted her arms to him again.

"What you're asking is a terrible thing, Jake. I never wanted serial monogamy. I have never dreamed of a life like that. I wanted love and marriage and children, to give them a real home like the one I've had." She swallowed, remembering that she was due to go home to her mother tomorrow. "And still have. I want that for my children. I want a man who wants that, too."

"I do want it!" he said, feeling the words were torn from him. "I do want it, but if I'm not capable of it, what is the point in pretending?"

She shook her head helplessly. "Marriage is what two people decide it will be, Jake, don't you realize that? I believe that if you decide that marriage is for life, then you make it that. And if you don't believe it possible, then it will be a self-fulfilling prophecy."

"People aren't always what they want to be," he said. "They aren't even what they think they are."

''Maybe,'' she agreed. She shrugged. He realized he was hurting her again, and shook his head in self-disgust. ''Can I call you?'' he asked.

She really didn't know what she wanted, what she would decide, what she could bear. But the thought of not hearing Jake's voice was too much to take right now. Maybe with time she would get used to it.

''Yes, all right.''

He reached to draw her to her feet, changed his mind, and instead turned and went up the steps to the door. ''See you,'' he said.

He opened the door on the words. Wind and rain crashed and roiled into the room, almost tearing the door from his grasp.

She looked away. She did not want to watch him leave.

''See you, Jake,'' she replied, but her words were lost. When the wind's howl was abruptly cut off, she knew she was alone.

Bel spent the weekend with her family, but she did not derive the solace she had wanted, or the comfort she was used to getting there. This time, when her father sat and talked with her younger brother, as well as seeing a father talking with his son, she saw something Jake would never do with their son. And when her mother threw her father a look because of something he said, in addition to seeing two people who had the knack of disagreeing lovingly, and a bond that had lasted nearly thirty years, she saw something which she would never have with Jake.

And if she could not have it with Jake, she didn't see how she would ever have it. The impersonal was no longer a comfort. She could not tell herself anymore that one day she would have a marriage like this, when the only man she had ever wanted, ever would want, could not give her a marriage like this.

So every gentle, loving touch or word between her parents became a brand that burned her with regret and longing, when always before such things had been a comfort and a sign of hope to her, even in her worst moments.

On Saturday night, her mother listened as she told her grief, but did not reassure her.

"Bel, if there's one thing I've learned in my life, it's that men don't change. A woman who marries a man hoping that she'll be able to change him is asking for a whole cartload of misery. You have to take your man as you find him, or not at all."

This stern truth brought the tears, never very far from the surface, flooding up. "But people do change! Everybody changes! Alcoholics go to Alcoholics Anonymous and give it up forever, don't they?"

Her mother nodded. "Yes, but I have never yet heard that anyone who went to AA because they were pushed by someone else ever made it work. They have to want it for themselves."

"You nagged Daddy to quit smoking and he did! I remember!"

Her mother shook her head. "Your father did not give up smoking because I nagged him about it. He gave it up because he started to have symptoms of asthma. You know how your grandfather suffers with his asthma. Your father was frightened he would get full-blown asthma if he kept smoking."

She spoke with such a calm lack of resentment that Bel stared at her, seeing a glimpse of something she had never understood before. "I always thought he did it for you."

"If life were that easy, Bel."

"So you think Jake would end up cheating on—on me?"

"Bel, he's *telling* you he will. What I'm saying is, you should take that into account when you make your decision."

The tears ran freely down her face. "I thought you would say love would…would…"

"If Jake had come to you to say, here are the risks, but I want to change, I want you and I promise if you marry me I'll work on myself—" She held up her hands. "That's not what he said, though, is it?"

"He said he wanted to, but he didn't believe he could change because his genes were against him."

Her mother raised her eyebrows in an expressive shrug, and Bel, who had been unconsciously hoping that her mother could fix this as she had fixed most problems in Bel's young life, suddenly found nothing between herself and despair. She put her arms on the table, laid her face on her arms, and wept hopelessly.

Of course they talked it over again and again, all through the weekend. Of course they discussed it from every possible angle. She learned things about her parents' marriage that surprised and even shocked her.

But in the end, the choice was the same—give up all her dreams for Jake, or give up Jake.

Dear Jake,
I'm writing this. I'm sorry, but I don't think I could talk about it and make any sense.

I can't do what you ask. I love you, and right now it feels as if I will never love anyone again the way I love you. And I guess if all the stories are true I won't.

However long we lasted together it would still kill

me when you left me, I know that. It's so hard to explain in words, but I guess you'll understand what I mean—I don't think I could ever find happiness again if and when that happened. If I say no now, I think there's some chance that in the future I'll have another chance at happiness with someone.

Not what I would have with you. I'll never feel like this again for anyone. But not everybody who has a happy marriage started out crazy in love. That's what my mother said and I think she's right.

I'm crazy in love with you, Jake. I wish, oh, Jake, I wish...

I don't want to talk to you. I can't talk to you. Please don't try to phone or see me. I've made my decision and I want to stick to it.

I know I'll love you all my life. I know that. And I'll always hope you're happy, whatever that takes for you.

Annabel

She supposed he got the letter, but he gave no sign.

Twelve

Tallia and Brad returned. The house was virtually finished, and they were both delighted with the result. But Tallia's first look at her sister made her eyes widen, and as soon as she could she got Bel alone to demand, in a horrified voice, "Bel, what's happened to you? What's the matter?"

She could survive when everything around her was impersonal. She had dealt with workmen and designers and deliverymen without cracking. But of course the loving concern in her sister's voice destroyed all that in a second. Bel's pale, drawn face crumpled, and her throat was torn with a hoarse sob that was horrible to hear.

"Don't ask, Tal!" she begged, fighting to get her voice back under some control. "Let's talk about it later. Not now."

Tallia took a deep, troubled breath. "Has someone hurt you? I have to know that, Bel," she said, when Bel tried to protest. "I can't go around oohing and aahing—please tell me what it is!"

"It's Jake," Bel whispered, and then the hot tears that had been her companion every night for long nights past burned their familiar way down her cheeks.

"*Jake?*" Tallia's turquoise eyes opened in angry, uncomprehending horror. "*What did he do to you?*"

"Nothing, nothing!" Bel said hastily. She tried to explain, but because she was trying to be brief, her words only confused her sister.

"He wants you to share him with other women?"

"No, not right now. But he thinks he might, in the future—"

At last she made Tallia understand. "I never heard of anything so awful in my life," said the new bride, in the full confidence of her husband's love and the early perfect joy of togetherness. But she quickly realized that her indignation only deepened Bel's pain, and she gave up exclaiming and wrapped her sister in her arms.

"Oh, Bel, I'm so sorry! I had no idea he was like that. I would never have pushed you two together if I'd thought he was. Oh, and it's all my fault—I kept inviting you to dinner together, and I made you drive with him, and then you had to sit beside him at the wedding...."

"It's not your fault. It would have happened sooner or later. He's Brad's friend—we were going to run into each other, weren't we?" Bel said. It felt as if they had been destined to meet, the bond between them was so strong, so it was stupid for Tallia to blame herself.

"Can I do anything to help? Can Brad talk to him?"

"The best thing you can do is not to try to bring us together. I don't want to see him. I know you have to invite him to parties and dinners, I mean, he's Brad's best friend, but please don't get upset if I won't come to see you if he's here. Please don't ever let me come and find him here unexpectedly."

"Oh, Bel, I didn't mean for it to be like this!" Tallia said despairingly. "I hoped—I knew he was really attracted to you, and I thought how nice it would be if…"

But she had to accept that that particular dream would not come true. It was one thing that not all Brad's money could buy for her.

There were other dreams that money could buy. As Tallia and Bel and Brad toured the offices and the guest house, Tallia told her what she had dreamed up.

"I left this room empty, because I didn't really understand whether the house was going to be for staff or a guest house or what," Bel explained in the second bedroom, as they admired her work on the little house. "I wasn't sure what you wanted. It could be a study or a child's bedroom or—"

"What I'd love, little sister, is if you would come and live here permanently," Tallia said. She threw her tall, handsome husband a look of loving gratitude that tore at Bel's heart.

"Oh, Tallia, I don't know if I—" she began, but Tallia interrupted urgently.

"Don't say no till you hear it all! Bel, I'd like you to work with me, too."

Bel's mouth dropped open. "What could I do to help you? I only took the requisite one course in science and that was astronomy two twelve!"

"You could put your English to good use writing up my experiments and—oh, there's lots you can do. Brad and I planned it all out, and it's not as if it would be a sinecure or anything. There really is a job there, Bel. Please say you'll take it!"

* * *

So she had something else to think about. Bel couldn't
answer right away, though she would have been thrilled
with the offer if only Jake were not Brad's best friend. It
would have been a perfect refuge, a place and a time to
lick her wounds and repair. But nowhere that Jake would
have regular access could be a refuge. And she had to think
of drawbacks that wouldn't have crossed her mind otherwise.

It was a long drive into the city, where most of her
friends were. Her social life would be difficult, she could
easily come to be dependent on Brad and Tallia for too
much. And Brad and Tallia were so in love it hurt her eyes
to watch them, as if they were a too-bright light.

Jake was Brad's best friend. Of course he would be
invited to the house often. How would she feel in her perfect little house, knowing that Jake was only yards away?
How could she stand it?

But in the end it wasn't considerations like this that
decided her. She made up her mind at dinner on Brad and
Tallia's second night home. Of course she had sat at their
table many times in the past, in Brad's penthouse apartment down in the city. And of course Brad and Tallia had
been in love then....

But something new had entered their relationship. They
were married now, they had a home they had chosen and
designed together, and in which their children would be
born. There was a whole new dimension to their happiness.
They planned together even without realizing they were
doing it. "When we..." filled their conversation without
either of them knowing it.

And Bel was the death's head at this feast of love. They
felt awkward, even guilty, being so happy when she was
so miserable. Because of course Tallia had told Brad about

it. And they would throw her anxious little glances when they talked about their future, and she knew she had to go.

"Aw, Bel!" Tallia cried when she told her. "Oh, I don't want you to go away and be all by yourself."

"I'll have friends in Vancouver, Tal. Quite a few will be coming back when the summer's over. Maybe I'll get someone to room with me, help with the rent."

"But you will take the job? I mean, you'd be driving against the traffic both ways, so that won't be a big problem. And Jake won't ever be here during working hours."

Bel hadn't thought of splitting up Tal's offer. So this was another decision in the long line of painful decisions she had had to make lately.

"Look," Tal said, when she hesitated. "You're going to have to stay here for another week or so, anyway, right?" Bel had sublet her apartment in the city to a summer student, and it wouldn't be hers again till September. "Why not start doing the job as a temporary thing, just to see if you like it? If it turns out you don't—" Tallia shrugged "—what have we lost?"

So that was how it was settled.

The noise of screaming tires and roaring engines blew across the pool as Jake squatted in front of the patio fridge. He grabbed out two cans of beer and tossed one to Brad as he straightened and sank into his chair.

"Pity about Villeneuve," Brad said.

"Yeah."

It was like old times, only it wasn't. Brad was different. He looked contented. His edge was gone.

Jake should have felt sorry for him, a guy who'd lost his edge, but he didn't. He envied him. Brad had made the transition from past to future without any soul-searching, with no sign of the deep-seated fear of his ability to change direction that plagued Jake.

The thing that Jake had never taken sufficiently into consideration was that a person changes. He'd figured he would always be the same, just getting older physically. He had never figured on the psychological changes that were happening to him with age. Like this weird feeling that he wanted to love and cherish one particular person. Like wanting children.

"So—Tallia pregnant yet?" he asked, pretending to watch as Hakkinen hugged the curves.

"No, we're waiting a year," Brad said comfortably. "Tallia's got a new project on, and we want to enjoy ourselves a bit more on our own first. We really like travelling and we're going to do more of that this year. Tallia wants to see India."

There was an easy possessiveness in his voice, the tone of a man whose right and duty it is to look after this particular woman. It made Jake aware that he had no such right or duty around Bel.

"Right." Jake nodded. "Sounds good."

"I hear you and Bel won't be an item after all."

Jake took a pull on his beer. "No, guess not."

There was a long pause while, on the screen, a struggle went on for lead position. Somebody lost a tire and went off the track in a cloud of dust and smoke.

Brad said, "So, what's going on there, Jake? What are you doing?"

Jake took another long pull of beer. The Ferrari logo roared by and he stared at the little screen as if entranced. Brad didn't speak again, and he felt the pressure build up. It was a familiar technique and he was annoyed with himself for succumbing. He shrugged.

"C'mon, Brad, you know I've never been the marrying kind. So what else is new?"

"Jake, you're not twenty anymore. You're not even thirty. And Bel's a great kid. Gorgeous and a brain, too. What more do you want?"

"She deserves better."

"That's a cop-out. Tallia says you told her you love her. That's not like you, to string anyone a line. She'll get hurt. She *is* hurt. Why'd you do it? I've never heard that you said that to a woman. Tallia thinks you said it just to get her into bed."

"Bel doesn't think that," Jake said flatly, and then, "Does she?" He looked over at Brad. "Does Bel think that?"

Brad shrugged. "Why *did* you tell her?"

Jake sighed irritably. "I told her because it's true and I was too stupid to lie about it. You're right, I shouldn't have told her if I'm not going to do the logical thing about it."

"Aren't you?"

Jake sat in silence while a half dozen cars in close formation screamed around a hairpin turn. He drained his beer, cradled the can in his hands hanging loosely between his knees and stared absently down at it.

"No," he said at last, and with a convulsive movement twisted up and fired the can towards the garbage can nestled in a corner of the patio. "No," he repeated in self-disgust, "I am not going to do anything about it, if by doing something you mean marriage."

"Why not?"

Jake picked up the remote and killed the sound of the race. He turned towards Brad. "Brad, I have history against me. My father cheats on my mother, my grandfather cheated on two wives. It's not something I want to get into. There's too much risk of hurting someone.''

''C'mon, Jake, that's a cop-out and you know it. That's just an excuse. You're afraid to take the risk.''

Jake grunted at the injustice of this, but found no answer.

''Everything's a risk, Jake. There are no guarantees, whoever your father was. You have to make the leap against some personal weakness, that's the nature of the beast.''

''What beast?''

''Life.'' Brad paused, shrugged. ''Being human, I guess. It's—if you don't take risks, Jake, you get stuck. Come on, she's my sister-in-law, and you're my friend, and we can't even put the two of you in the same room together.''

For some reason, that made his head ache. ''Did Bel say that?''

''Of course she said it. It's going to put a hell of a crimp in our style, and it's upsetting Tallia, too.''

''She'll get over it. She's better off without me,'' Jake said doggedly.

''That's just fear talking.''

''Am I hearing the guy whose hand I had to hold all through our stock market investments?''

''Emotional risk is a lot scarier than financial risk. What the hell difference does it make what your father did, or your grandfather? You're your own man.''

''Look who's talking!'' Jake exclaimed, feeling goaded. ''Who's the guy who wouldn't date an actress because his mother left him for Hollywood when he was three?''

''I married her in the end, Jake, in case you hadn't noticed.''

There was a silence. ''Yeah, but Tallia's not an actress anymore, is she?'' Jake knew he sounded like someone grasping at straws, which really pissed him off, because he wasn't. He knew what he was doing was right.

"You think there's no risk there, a woman as beautiful as Tallia? That she'll never be tempted to go back to it?"

Jake blinked. "God, do you really think there's a possibility of that? I thought she hated all that stuff."

"People change. Nobody comes with a written guarantee. That includes Tallia. But she was worth the risk. If you're wondering, marrying her was the best thing I've ever done. I…" Words failed him. "I can personally recommend marriage."

"Brad, that was you taking the risk of getting hurt yourself," Jake said, fighting to the last ditch. "The choice I'm faced with is taking a risk that one day I'll hurt Annabel. There's a big difference."

Brad gazed at him, shaking his head at this verbal fast footwork.

"Whose behaviour is going to be easier to control, Jake? Your own or someone else's? You can decide, if you want to, that you will never cheat on Annabel." He moved his shoulders impatiently.

"Come on, we're thirty-three. We're not going to be young forever. I want kids, Jake, and I'd like it if they grew up along with yours. With a little forward planning, we could build our own baseball team. There's a lot more to life than screwing around."

"I'm not screwing around."

Brad turned to stare at his buddy. *"What?"*

Jake leaned over, groped in the fridge and popped another beer. "I haven't been near any woman but Bel for months," he muttered.

Brad could scarcely believe his ears. His jaw slowly dropped open. "Then what the hell is the problem?"

Jake picked up the remote, and suddenly the patio was filled with the noise of protesting tires again.

Bel stood on the second-floor deck, looking out over the lawn, where little storm lanterns sparkled invitingly, watching as groups of Brad and Tallia's friends and family formed, broke and reformed.

She was nervous and uncomfortable, and wished that Tallia had not asked her to come. Tallia had promised her there would be at least eighty people, and it looked as though there were a lot more than that, but there was no safety in numbers tonight.

She was nervous and unhappy, her nerves stretched to snapping. She was hoping he would not come, that he would find some excuse, but that didn't prevent her jumping every time the bell rang or a car drew in to the parking area.

She wasn't looking good, and she knew it, which was another reason not to see him. She had lost weight. She wasn't sleeping and her eyes had dark circles. Her skin had lost its tan. She looked pale and unhealthy.

She didn't want to meet Jake tonight. Not when he would see at a glance how desperately she was suffering. She peered at her watch and wondered how soon she could leave without hurting Tallia's feelings.

She wondered again if Jake had arrived yet. She was hiding up here, really, because she was so terrified of entering any room in case he was there.

Besides herself, there was only one couple on the deck now, and Bel suddenly came to and realized that they would prefer to be alone.

She slid open the door, stepped into the darkened room behind, and almost walked into Jake. She gasped, jerked back instinctively, then got herself under control. "Hello," she said.

She was about to step to one side around him, feeling that she wanted to pick up her skirt and run, but he spoke.

"Annabel. I see you were able to face the possibility of being in the same room with me."

She didn't understand his anger. She shrugged. Her heart was suddenly beating wildly enough to choke her. "I guess we'll have to get used to it sooner or later."

He shook his head. "I don't have anything to get used to. It doesn't offend me to see you. You're the one who put an embargo on our meeting or talking. You're the one who won't come to dinner if I'm invited."

Bel began to feel like one who is unjustly accused. "And are you surprised at that? I told you—"

"You don't want a relationship with me! Fine! But it's a bit extreme to refuse to be in the same room with me."

"*You* are the one who doesn't want a relationship, Jake. You—"

She stopped speaking as people entered the room. Jake took her arm and dragged her to a darkened corner.

"That is not the case and you know it," he ground out, struggling to keep his voice low. "I offered you anything you wanted, including marriage, but it comes with a warning. You're the one who wants guarantees no human being could possibly give!"

The heat of his anger astonished her, his injustice enraged her.

"I did not ask for a guarantee! I never mentioned guarantee! All I wanted to hear from you was—"

"You wanted promises! You wanted it on the dotted line. In this day and age that's like asking for the moon and you know it."

"No, it's not! Not for someone—"

"Fifty percent of marriages end in divorce. How can I promise to buck the odds? That's—"

"Who's talking about the half-empty glass now, Jake?" she cried angrily.

In the gloom she saw him blink with surprise. "What do you mean?"

"Half of all marriages end in divorce, Jake. What about the other half?"

He was silent.

"The other half of all marriages *don't* end in divorce!"

"And you think you can decide which half you'll end up in?"

"Yes, I do," Bel said flatly.

"And because I don't, that's the end of you and me, am I right?"

"Jake, that isn't how it was."

"That is exactly how it was. I came and asked you to— I told you I loved you and I said I'd marry you. And your answer to this is to send me a letter—a two-hundred-and-thirty-two word letter," he rasped, his voice hoarse with feeling, "telling me not to try to contact you. And you even tell Brad and Tallia you won't be in the same room with me. True or not, Bel?"

"Jake—"

"True or not?"

She was every bit as mad as he was now. "Not true!" she bit out, still in an undervoice, though the new arrivals had hastily abandoned the room almost as soon as they entered it. "Not true! You put all the responsibility onto me. I can take responsibility for my own share of things, Jake, but not the whole thing. There comes a point where everybody has to stand up and be counted, and you were sitting down when your turn came. Okay, that's your choice, that's your right. But don't you—"

She was waving a finger at him, and he grabbed her wrist and pulled her against him. The words on her lips died with a gasp.

"I love you," he said angrily. "I love you and want to live with you, on any terms you care to name. Why is that not good enough?"

"You *know* why."

His other arm slipped behind her back so that she felt trapped. Her senses were dizzy.

"Why won't you let me make love to you again? It won't be anything like it was that day. Why won't you let me, Bel? Dammit, I love you! I want you! I want to make it right with you. I could convince you if you would only let me…'

His body was growing hard against hers; hers was melting against his.

"Jake, this isn't fair. You—"

"Fair! How the hell can you talk about what's fair? Dammit, I am going up the walls, and you won't even eat dinner with me. What the hell has fair got to do with it?"

"Jake—"

"Come home with me. Come home with me now," he said urgently.

Suddenly the lights went on, blinding them. "Oh, sorry!" someone said. "I was looking for—"

"Well, it's not in here!" Jake said loudly, and there was a stifled gasp from the offending party and the lights immediately went out again.

"Sorry!" said the voice, and footsteps hurried away.

"Come home with me!" Jake said again.

Bel drew a shaking breath. "What's changed, Jake?"

"Nothing's changed. I still love you and want you and I'm still willing—"

"Nothing's changed," she interrupted him flatly. She

shook her head. "It's still you get what you want exactly the way you want it. And I get—what do I get? A better time in bed than you showed me before?"

His hold tightened. "Bel!"

But she straightened, and he had to let her go. "Not on these terms, Jake," she said sadly.

And then she turned and walked away.

Thirteen

Bel paced the floor, hugging herself, weeping. The nights were always worst, the hardest to get through. She dreaded nights, like tonight, when she knew in advance she would not sleep.

She had moved back into her apartment. Here at least there were no memories of Jake. Brad and Tallia's place had been haunted by him. Every room had been touched by his presence, she had a memory of him everywhere, and her bedroom, which should have been her place of refuge, was worst of all.

She had expected to be freer of him in her own place, but she was not. Now she was tormented by the fact that they were so close, geographically. Nearly every night she felt the yearning to go to him, so strong that she could not understand how he could resist the compulsion to come to her.

She could not go to him. To go to him meant giving in,

meant accepting that he would never give her anything but sexual pleasure, meant never being able to ask for more. If he came to her, that would be a sign of some crack in his resistance, his fear of commitment…if she went to him he might never break through.

And then one day he would leave her. And she would be no better off then than she was right now. Worse off, probably. She could not go to him. It would be the ruin of all her hopes for a real future with him.

But he could come to her. If he was unhappy without her, the solution was in his hands…but she didn't even know if he was unhappy without her. He had been, of course, but now? He had an out that she didn't—he might already have gone back to his usual life and wiped out her memory with other women's faces.

She tried to send him mental messages. *Please come. Please find you can't live without me. Please find commitment in your heart.*

"I don't believe it," Jake said, shaking his head in helpless resignation.

The brunette smiled at him speculatively. It was clear from the light in her eyes that she liked what she saw. "What don't you believe?"

"Patchouli," he said.

She cocked an inquiring eyebrow at him.

"You're wearing Patchouli."

"And?"

He shrugged. "Whenever I think there's something special about a woman," he said, smiling lazily into her eyes, "it usually turns out she's wearing Patchouli."

"Really?"

He indicated yes with his dark eyebrows, not breaking their locked gaze. "Now why would that be?"

He was determined to get back in the running. After his conversation with Brad he had felt challenged. Well, threatened. He didn't know by what, exactly, but he figured that the solution was to be found in his old, comfortable habits. And after his argument with Bel he was angry enough for anything.

"I don't know. They say moths can smell their mates over a distance of hundreds of miles. Maybe you're related to a moth," the brunette drawled.

Jake laughed. Now that was a remark almost worthy of Bel. That dry refusal to take a comment personally, to fall for a line. Bel was so levelheaded, and yet... Jake put a brake on his thoughts and returned to the here and now.

She felt lost, a ship that has sailed for a safe haven only to find that, instead of entering a port where it can rest, it has sailed through a channel out into a stormy ocean.

Love was supposed to be the one safe thing in the world. She had always believed that when she found love, she would be safe. Well, she had found love, but for her it was not safe. It was full of danger and pain and risk and unhappiness.

If love wasn't safe, what was safe in life?

She was being buffeted, tossed on terrible seas, and there was no light to guide her, no sight of land.

Sometimes she believed that she would never be happy again. Nights were worst. Then she was alone with the universe, with no distractions. Then she would wander up and down in her apartment, hugging herself, fighting not to phone him, not to go to him, waiting for morning.

This part of it had been easier at Brad and Tallia's. There, when she had a bad night, she had gone outside and wandered around the lawn and pool, gazing over at the city where Jake was, or up at the stars, which proved to her how small this problem was in the scheme of things.

> *...then on the shore*
> *Of the wide world I stand alone and think*
> *Till Love and Fame to nothingness do sink.*

She had recited such words to herself, and although love never yet had sunk to nothingness with her, out under the stars she could believe that one day it would, or how could the poet write that it did? And she would get some comfort from that.

But here in her apartment she could only stand by the windows and stare out at the wet, darkened street and the building opposite, against a low black sky whose stars were hidden from her. She wanted to walk, to burn off this agony, to feel the wind in her hair and the rain on her face, but she wasn't such a fool that she thought she could go wandering around the streets of the city at this hour.

Why didn't he come? How could he stand the separation? It was beyond bearing. "Jake," she wept, and paced again. "Jake, please, please come to me."

"Are you an entomologist?"

Always assume a solid, significant career. It flattered women who didn't have one as well as those who did.

She chuckled. "No, I happened to read about moths in the paper."

She was interested, challenging him a little to keep him on his mettle. The problem was, Jake realized abruptly, *he* wasn't interested. He'd sat around for more than an hour before he saw her, too. He wasn't sure why he'd suddenly decided she was the one.

But it didn't matter. He was going to go through with this. He had to prove something.

It had been a long time—years—since he'd hung out in clubs and bars. For a long time now he had met women professionally, through some aspect of his work: doctors, brokers, other lawyers. Committed career women, he'd found, tended to be looking for no more than he was in a relationship. Happy to spend time in a non-exclusive relationship and then move on.

Or at least that had been true till a couple of years ago, when quite a few of the women he met, passing the thirty mark, had started to hear their body clocks ticking. They tended to move on very quickly. Like Bel. Only she hadn't even stopped. She had just passed right on by.

Well, and that was the smart thing to do, he had to admit that. He'd been angry, but he had no right to be. He accepted that now. A woman like her, looking for what she was looking for—he had absolutely nothing to offer her. Because for her a short-term romance was nothing.

He understood that now.

"So, what do you do?" the brunette asked.

She touched the phone, and his number ran unbidden through her mind. She had never dialled it, but she had let herself get as far as looking it up once, just once. And now it was burned into her memory, tempting her with its ease of access in moments like this.

No.

She looked at the clock. Hours till dawn, and for sure she would not sleep till then. Oh, God, how was she meant to get through this night?

She could drive, she realized suddenly. She would be safe enough in the car. She could drive down to the sea wall and sit with her window open...or even drive up into the mountains. She might find a hotel when morning came, and spend the weekend away.

She wouldn't choose a destination now. She would let the spirit move her. Bel grabbed a small overnight bag and tossed a few necessaries into it, then took her handbag and keys and quietly let herself out. Down in the garage she flung her bag into the car, feeling with this release from the prison of her apartment a sudden burst of energy. She locked herself in and drove out into the street, where the street lamps glistered in the light rain.

He hadn't wanted to phone any of the numbers in his book, though he knew he could have found someone on the loose who was willing to have a quick reprise for old time's sake. He hadn't wanted the cool, almost impersonal friendliness, the matter-of-fact bedroom gossip about various colleagues or recent court decisions.

He didn't know what he did want, but he had come to the club hoping to find it. After all these years, the club was still a place where professional singles hung out, but he was surprised at how young most of them were. Hell, most of them looked younger than Bel.

"Spritzer, please," the brunette said as the waitress paused by the table, and he suddenly realized that she looked like Bel. Long brown hair, slim but firm build, cheekbones, small chin...but much more knowing. Not someone he would have to wonder if she was a virgin...

Jake sat up with a jolt. And just like that, as if a land mine had suddenly been triggered in his head, he saw it. Saw what he wanted, saw what he had to do to get it.

Everything's a risk, it's the nature of the beast.

I can't take responsibility for your decision, Jake.

"Do you want another?" prompted the brunette, but he

didn't take it in, and only shook his head, frowning, thinking. The waitress, taking this as her signal, departed.

He was backing up. That was why he was bored. He would never find what he wanted here, because what he really wanted was the power to change, to move forward.

He wanted to be worthy of Bel. He wanted to win her.

"What's the matter?" asked a voice.

He stared at the brunette and realized at last what he was doing, what risk he was running here. All the wrong kind. The risk of being a guy on the prowl forever, looking for younger and younger women...

The choice opened in front of him, a chasm with only one narrow, dangerous bridge. The bridge was a terrifying prospect. If he tried to cross it, he might fall. It might break and fling him to his doom.

But on the other side of that bridge, Bel was waiting for him.

If he *didn't* try to cross the bridge, his future was certain—the abyss.

It was all so clear. Everybody had seen it but himself. *It's a risk, it's always a risk.*

If it hadn't been his fear of his grandfather's genes, it would have been some other fear. That was what Brad had been trying to tell him. *It's the nature of the beast.*

If you don't go forward, you go back. His father had said that all his life. If he didn't go forward now, he lost Bel and his future children, and his own maturity. He had seen them, hanging around the clubs, the aging roués, the Casanovas...when he was a kid such men had always made him and his friends uncomfortable, though he couldn't have said why—then.

They had preyed on girls, tried to join groups of kids half their age, had picked up all the freshest slang so as not to appear out of date...but they had fooled no one but themselves.

Guys who had missed the boat and didn't know it.

Jake's boat was about to leave. She had blown the whistle. Hell, he might already be too late. He had wasted so much time....

He was on his feet almost without realizing it.

"What's the matter?" someone asked again.

He came to and focussed on the brunette. She seemed like something out of another life.

"I'm afraid I have to get back to the office."

"The *office?* At this hour?"

"I'm waiting for a call from the Middle East. I just dropped in for a quick drink while I waited."

She went a little stiff as the implication sank in. "Well, the jinx is broken, anyway."

"The jinx?"

She lifted her head and stared at him from angry, half-shut eyes. "Yeah, you know, the one where you always score with women wearing Patchouli."

The sea was flat and dead calm, the way it often was during a light rain. Bel sat for a while watching the drops of rain freckle the blackness, watching how the lights of the city, reflecting from the surface, fractured and regrouped with a slight swell.

She rolled her window down and sat in silence, not wanting to put her radio on for fear of attracting some of the other night wanderers who were certainly out there: those who wanted to exchange tales of misery, mostly, but also some who might want to deal out a share of misery to any chance-met soul....

A police car cruised slowly by along the sea wall. She

felt the pause, the registering of her presence, and then it moved on.

She sat for fifteen minutes or so, trying not to think of anything, wishing she could risk taking a stroll by the water, before a shadow moved stealthily under the trees on her right and she knew it would be wiser to move.

She rolled up her window, started her engine quietly and backed up to the street before putting on her lights and pulling away.

There was little traffic, the hour and the rain keeping people indoors. She drove at random, thinking about heading for the bridge and up into the mountains—or even just to Brad and Tallia's place, where she could probably spend the night in the guest house without disturbing them.

But she did not turn the car that way yet. She drove through the quietest streets, the residential areas where trees lined the road, without any conscious intent, heading she knew not where, until she caught sight of a street sign and realized where she was.

She was only a few minutes away from Jake's place.

Fourteen

—

"Jake!" cried his mother, whirling. "What a nice surprise!"

He had entered the kitchen by the back door.

"Hi, Mom," he said, slipping an arm around her waist and bending to kiss her offered cheek. He felt the familiar burst of protectiveness that had first assailed him when he was seventeen or eighteen and had suddenly realized that he was taller, bigger and stronger than his mother.

"It's late for a visit. Is something wrong?" she asked.

"Making some of your soup?" he asked, avoiding the question. He reached over her to lift a lid. A pot of thick simmering broth met his eyes. "Mmmm!" he said appreciatively.

His mother glanced into his face but said nothing.

"Jake! Hiya, man! How's it going?" Knowing his duty, Jake turned and slapped palms with his young brother Saul, the product of a late miscalculation of his mother's fertility on the part of his parents. "I saw your car in the driveway! I'm glad I wasn't asleep!"

"I'd like to know why you weren't!" his mother observed dispassionately.

Saul grinned. "Hey, Jake, will you come upstairs and—"

Jake held up his hand. "I need to talk to Dad, Saul. Catch you another time, okay?"

"Tomorrow? Are you going to spend the night?"

"Not sure, Saul."

"Well, if you do, remember I'm next in line! Don't let Oliver come along and hijack you, it's my turn next!" Saul said.

"Bed, Saul," said his mother inexorably, flicking another glance at her eldest son.

"As long as Jake remembers he's mine next!" Saul complained, going.

"Why do I feel like a commodity?" Jake murmured.

"Because you don't come home nearly often enough."

Jake opened his eyes at the injustice of this. "Mom, I'm here every couple of weeks or so!"

"I rest my case. And anyway, it's a lot longer than that since you were here last. Have you eaten?"

Jake nodded.

"If you want beer, there's some in the fridge." She returned to the vigorous chopping of onions.

Jake pulled open the fridge and grabbed a beer, opened it, then flung himself into a familiar, comfortable pose in a chair by the kitchen table, the way he had done all his childhood. He hadn't done it for years, but it all came back to him as if he had been here last week.

He wondered if one day his kids would feel the same way about Bel's kitchen.

"So," his mother began, just as if these heart-to-hearts

had never suffered a hiatus. "That was a wonderful wedding. Isn't Tallia a lovely girl? Brad's very lucky!"

He took a pull on his Labatt's. "Yeah," said Jake. "Gorgeous."

Barbara Drummond smiled. "Her sister's pretty special, too, I understand."

Jake frowned at his mother. "Who were you talking to, Mom?" he demanded suspiciously.

"Her Aunt Miranda."

"Not Brad?"

She gave him a look. "Not surprisingly, Miranda had the idea that your attentions meant something special. I did my best to disabuse her mind of that idea..."

"Oh, you did."

"But some women, you know, live on hope. I told her I'd been waiting and hoping for years, but she just kept insisting that rakes make good husbands when they reform, and it certainly seemed to her that—what was her name?"

"Annabel," he supplied automatically. His mother bent lower over the onions for a moment, and when she spoke, he could hear she was smiling.

"Annabel!—was in a fair way to reforming you! She said she recognized the signs."

He swore.

"Don't get rude. Miranda is a very nice woman who means well. Her only failing, as far as I could see, is a determination to pair up the entire human population and marry them off to each other. Which some among us, of course, would not consider a failing, exactly. If it worked."

"Was she wearing a blue hat?" Jake asked, frowning.

"Oh, dear, such a long time ago...yes, maybe."

"She kept smirking at me."

"That would be Miranda. I told her you couldn't be

more adamantly set against marriage. But I have to say, as a not quite impartial observer who has, after all, seen you with any number of…should we say, pretty young women?…over the years, that you didn't seem precisely detached when Brad's friend Jordan asked Annabel to slow dance. That's the first time I've seen you do *that*.'

Jake took a drink. ''Yeah, well, we all bite the dust sooner or later, Mom,'' he said.

He counted only as far as two. Onions, knife, cutting board all clattered onto the floor as his mother whirled to face him, her mouth wide with astonishment and delight.

''Jake!'' she cried. ''Oh, *Jake!* Really?''

She covered the space between them in a nanosecond and wrapped him in a bear hug. ''Is it Annabel? Is it really? It looked like it, but I just didn't dare to hope! Such a gorgeous girl! And a lovely family! Oh, and Brad's wife's sister, too! Oh, I'm so happy!''

She babbled and wiped hasty tears. He answered a few questions, but although he didn't know it, there was a frown of worry on his brow, and at last his mother drew back and merely looked at him.

''What is it, Jake?''

He shook his head. ''She hasn't accepted yet, Mom. I might have left it too late to… Dad around? I'd kinda like to talk to him.''

She didn't worry him with questions, and he thought, not for the first time, that she was a mother in a million.

''He's in the garage setting up that potting wheel and kiln your great-uncle gave us. You can give him a hand. Your father has never been quite as adept at mechanical things as he thinks. Come in later for some soup if you want to.''

It couldn't hurt to drive past, she told herself. She could just look at the house, she didn't have to stop or anything, could just see whether the lights were on or not. See if he was awake. Maybe if he was having a party or something she would catch a glimpse of him on the doorstep as he said goodbye to friends.

The house was in darkness. Probably he wasn't even at home. It wouldn't hurt just to pull up and look at the place, how could that hurt? It didn't mean she was giving in. He would never even know.

Bel let the car coast to a stop and killed the engine. She had been here once before, months ago, before the wedding, when Tallia had asked her to drop something off. Of course it had been a deliberate attempt to get them together, but when he had asked her in and offered her a drink beside his pool she had shaken her head and almost run back to her car....

There wasn't a light, even over the front door. Nothing stirred. He probably wasn't even in, so it couldn't hurt to get out and just walk up to the front door and remember that day and wish that everything could be different....

A dog started barking next door and was hushed. She felt something push her ankle, and looked down to see a white cat, back arched and inviting, hoping her presence meant the door would open. So there were two of them waiting for him...but the cat had no other home. No place to go if Jake didn't come home and let it in.

Bel let out a little laugh. *She* had no other home. Her home was wherever Jake was.

With an uncontrollable urgency she pushed the bell. He wasn't home, the cat was evidence of that, but somehow the action relieved her feelings a little. She heard the peal of the bell inside, sounding impossibly loud in the darkness of the night, and bit her lip.

"Don't get your hopes up, kitty," she warned. "Probably you've got a lot longer to wait before he gets home. Not as long a wait as I'm facing, though. I might be waiting all my life.''

She hadn't voiced the fear before, and she was shocked by the power of tears and grief that came up behind the words. She gulped on a sob, and bit her lip. How stupid, to come apart at the seams because she had talked to Jake's cat! How pathetic she was!

The cat purred and pressed up against her shins with little leaps, encouraging her to stroke it, and she smiled down through her tears. ''Oh, cat!'' she murmured protestingly. She had the sudden impulse to bend and snatch the cat into her arms, and steal away with it. That way she would have something of Jake's....

She suddenly realized that the logical explanation for his absence at this hour was that he was in bed with someone. Pain stabbed her deep in the heart, and all the air rushed out of her body.

God, what if he had brought whoever it was home, and had answered the door and...how humiliating it would be if she had come to him, only to discover like that that he did not want her anymore! With a wordless cry, Bel turned and flung herself back down the walk and into her car.

When she pulled away the white cat was halfway down the walk, blinking after her and mewing.

''Pretty neat, eh?'' said Eliot Drummond. ''I'm hoping the young ones will take to it, and I'm going to take a beginners' pottery class myself. What the heck, at the very least it'll make for a good supply of Christmas presents. Ever done pottery yourself, Jake?''

''No, Dad.''

''You're an intuitive. Jung says it's important for intuitives to have a sensation outlet.''

"Jung!" Jake repeated resignedly, rolling his eyes.

"Carl Jung—you know, the psychologist. He was an intuitive—used to sculpt stone. It wouldn't hurt you to try pottery. Or carpentry."

"Yeah, Dad, I've heard this before," Jake said calmly. All his life, in fact. Carl Jung would always be the lynchpin of his father's philosophy, regardless of short-lived trends and deconstruction.

"You've heard it, but did you ever take it in?"

"Dad, do we have to talk about Carl Jung?"

His father pierced him with a look. "He was a great one for understanding moments of transition, Jake."

Jake jumped. However annoying his father was with his constant reference to the psychological—which was, after all, his profession—he did have the ability to startle his son with his insight from time to time.

"What makes you think—?"

"Hey, c'mon, this is your old man here! What's happened, you taking the plunge?"

Jake stared. Even by his father's standards, this was pretty good.

"Who's it going to be? The one we saw you with at the wedding? Annabel, was it?"

"Dad, how the hell do you know?" Jake asked, almost irritably. "I mean, are you a lucky guesser, or what?"

His father gave the potting wheel a tentative spin, then bent to another adjustment. "I watch patterns in human life, Jake. It's a natural progression, isn't it, for a young man to move from what you might call the general to the specific in his romantic attachments. A man gets to the point where he ceases to look merely for sexual gratification in a woman."

He stood and wagged the screwdriver at Jake. "Did you know that the Muslims say that the most important thing a man does for his children is choose their mother? There comes a moment, if he's smart, when a man starts looking at the world with that kind of slant.''

"And you just happened to guess that I'm at that point?"

"More than a guess, but don't ask me for all the details of what I've observed. So, do I congratulate you, or haven't you asked her yet?"

Jake took a long pull of his beer. "I haven't asked her yet. She—I think she'll say yes, even though I've told her what a risk I'd be as a husband. That's why I'm here." He looked at his father. "I want to know if you think I'm doing the right thing."

His father set down his screwdriver and straightened. "Jake, I've barely met the girl. Why don't you bring her out here for dinner before you ask my opinion? Anyway, what could I possibly tell—"

"I don't mean about Bel. I mean me. I mean... Do you think you did the right thing, marrying Mom?"

Eliot Drummond stared at his son. "I should knock you down for that. What the hell do you mean? We sweated our lives making this a happy, safe home for you, and you ask me if I think I did the right thing? What the hell's the matter with you?"

"Sorry, Dad. I didn't mean—" He broke off, because it was exactly what he had meant. "What I'm trying to say is, is it fair for men like us to marry, knowing what kind of genes we've inherited?"

His father crossed his arms, frowning, and leaned his shoulders against the wall. "What genes, exactly, are you referring to?"

Fifteen

"**G**randfather's, of course."

"*My* father?"

Jake shook his head impatiently and lifted a palm. "Look, Dad, you don't have to cover for him. I know all about him. I've known, like, since I was ten."

Eliot looked at his son. "You've known? What?"

"He was a playboy, and I inherited his genes. He should never have married, and I always figured I took after him and it would be a mistake if I did."

Eliot Drummond straightened, dropped his arms and gazed piercingly at his son.

"Sophia," he said unerringly.

Jake only nodded.

"I had no idea that your grandmother had poisoned your mind with all that crap. I thought she'd run her course with me."

"It's true, though, isn't it? He left her for Angela."

His father said levelly, "Yes, Dad left Mom for Angela.
And a bloody embittered woman my mother became because of it. She never was one to face an uncomfortable
truth."

Jake blinked. "But I thought—"

"She ever tell you the circumstances of her marriage,
Jake?"

"I don't remember."

He crossed his arms. "Dad and Mom married on No-
vember 20, 1939. Does that tell you anything?"

Jake racked his brain and came up with something.
"The war?" he asked, shrugging.

"That's right. Canada had declared war on Germany in
September. And Dad was in the reserves, did you know
that?"

"I can't remember if I knew that."

His father nodded. "When it became clear that the reserves were going to be sent overseas almost immediately,
your great-grandparents, God bless them, with the memory
of the First World War still fresh, decided that it would
be a good thing if Dad had someone soft and pretty here
at home to send him letters and cookies and knitted socks
for the duration while he sat and suffered in those cold
wet trenches.

"Someone to live for. So he married Sophia."

"What?" Jake whispered in disbelief.

"It was another time, Jake, another era."

Jake swore.

"He fell in love with Angela overseas, but he came back
here and I think he did his best to make the marriage work
for about six months. By then I was five or six, and
frankly, I didn't like having him around at all. He was
strict, a thing my mother never was.

"They didn't get along, either. The truth was, if he had

died on the battlefield, Mom would have been perfectly happy. It was only when he told her he wanted a divorce that…well, it was a question of pride, but she wouldn't admit that to herself. She made his life hell for a while, with tears and recriminations, and when he left she never let herself forget what he'd done. Or me.'' He shook his head. ''Or you, I guess.''

Jake stood silent, taking it in. Feeling inadequate to cope with this shifting world.

''Let's get outside,'' his father said, leading the way. ''I need some fresh air. Why didn't I realize she would talk to you exactly the same way she talked to me? She never was a woman to learn from her mistakes, or grow emotionally. She was stuck in anger and resentment.''

Father and son emerged into the damp night and found seats on the picnic table beside the pool.

''Let me have a pull of that beer,'' said his father, reaching for it and suiting the action to the word.

''So, what did she tell you about yourself?'' he demanded, wiping his lip. He passed the beer back.

Stumblingly, Jake tried to express the sense of his masculine self that he had received at the hands of his grandmother Sophia. Since it was still nearly impossible for him to absorb the fact yet that this wasn't the plain truth, he felt his recital was a bit confused.

Also he felt as though his world was on its head. All his certainties had died. Never had he sounded less like his polished lawyer self.

''And…well, she said that I would be incapable of remaining faithful to a woman and so I—if I wanted to be decent, I should never get married,'' he finished.

His father reacted with barely controlled fury. ''That…!'' He cursed with a colourful and inventive violence of language that Jake had never before been privileged to hear from him.

"But you always said Grandpa was a rogue among women," Jake protested. "When I started dating you said yourself I took after him."

"Yes, it's true he was a bit of a rogue, and it's true I was, but once you make that choice to get married, Jake, you've outgrown it. You've changed."

Jake looked blank. "But—have you stopped cheating on Mom?"

The words were out of his mouth before he could recall them.

Eliot Drummond whirled on him in such ferocious amazement Jake leaned backwards. It was the first time he had ever been physically afraid of his father.

"Are you seriously looking to get knocked down? What the hell's gotten into you? I never cheated on your mother!"

There was silence, during which they each heard the sound of their breathing.

"Dad, I heard you," he said unwillingly at last. "I heard you and Mom arguing about it."

His father went still. He gave Jake a long, level look, and what was in his eyes now made his son acutely uncomfortable. There was a long pause while neither spoke. Then his father lowered his head and looked at his hands clasped between his knees.

"Jake, you told me you didn't come into the house that day. You swore you dumped your hockey stuff outside and went off with Neil and his dad." His voice sounded absolutely exhausted. He sounded like an old man.

Jake swallowed, feeling fifteen years old again, helpless, angry, sad, guilty, sorry for his mother. "I got as far as the living room. I heard—" He lifted a hand. "Mom was crying and you—I didn't stay, I turned around and snuck out. I went over to Brad's."

"And from that one incident you extrapolated a whole pattern of behaviour?"

"It was Grandma who told me it was…a regular thing with you. She said Mom put a brave face on it, and that was why she seemed so happy."

His father's hands clenched. "I will never understand her motives for—" He bit it off. "Well, I gave her the ammunition, but I wish I'd known it was you she was shooting with it!

"Once!" he said roughly, shaking his head. "Once, and it was the worst mistake I ever made! It was a stupid, meaningless—I was drunk! I no more meant to do it than blow up a bank! And I've never been sorrier for anything in my life, Jake. Take it from me, nothing is worth it! It took your mother I don't know how long to trust me again."

He paused.

"But she did, and she does, and she is right to trust me, Jake."

There was silence as they sat side by side staring across the pool while shadowy autumn leaves floated down and lighted gently on the surface of the water.

"I haven't closed the pool yet. I'll have to do it tomorrow," his father remarked absently.

"*Did* Grandpa ever cheat on Angela?" Jake asked.

"That's what your grandmother told you?"

Jake nodded, finished his beer and set down the can.

"Within a month of the wedding, according to her."

Eliot Drummond took a deep breath.

"Well, I don't think he ever did. I think that was a fantasy your grandmother built up because it made her feel better. You could always go and ask Angela."

"Pass."

"The truth is, Jake, that if genetics counts for anything in such matters, which I take leave to doubt, you come from a line of men who like women and enjoy the sexual game in youth, but who become model husbands and fathers if they're lucky enough to marry the right woman. Is Bel the right woman for you?"

"Yes."

His father looked over with a rueful grin. "Well, then, if my experience is anything to go by, you can consider your wings clipped. I have never felt the least inclination to risk all this—" his hand swept an arc that seemed to include not merely the physical house but his relationships with those within "—for the sake of casual sex with someone else.

"When I met your mother, I knew that was it for me."

In the east, behind the mountains, the sky was turning a lighter shade of navy by the time she returned home, and instead of driving into the garage she left the car on the street and went in the front entrance. The elevator was waiting and she stepped into it, suddenly feeling how exhausted she was.

She should consider herself lucky that on the night she had cracked he was out. Suppose he had been there? Suppose he had accepted her defeat and taken her to bed and made love to her and then told her that he was already seeing other women?

She was lucky, she knew it, but if that was true why was her heart being torn in two, making her pant like an animal in a trap?

As the doors closed and the elevator lifted, she felt her fragile control slip, and she leaned against the wall as sobs forced their way to the surface.

Then the doors opened at her floor and Jake was standing in front of her.

"Good morning," he said, in a voice that was raw with feeling. He looked over her shoulder into the elevator. "I see he had the good luck not to come home with you."

"Jake!"

Her voice was nothing but a breath. He reached for her and drew her out of the elevator into the hall, then shepherded her to her door. She fumbled with the keys until he took them from her and unlocked and opened the door and guided her inside.

Then he kicked the door shut and they stood staring at each other. She saw that his jaw was clenched tight, and his eyes were as dark and fathomless as the night sky.

"Who were you with, Bel?"

He was here. He had come to her. They had been looking for each other at the same time. The information slowly filtered in. She began to smile, and his jaw tightened and his eyes went bleak and grim.

"Am I too late, Bel?"

She swallowed and opened her mouth, but speech failed her. Her heart was pounding so hard it closed her throat.

"Tell me!" he almost shouted. "I've been here for hours, and I know you haven't been at Brad's because I phoned them!"

She couldn't stop smiling, but finally she could speak. "You locked your cat out, Jake," she told him softly. "She's sitting on the doorstep waiting to be let in, and it's been raining all night."

His eyes widened, and flame leapt up in them so fiercely that she caught her breath. He cried her name once as he understood, and in another second she was wrapped in his arms, his mouth was pressed against hers, and she was being half-dragged, half-lifted down the hall towards the bedroom, and into the darkness within.

He didn't lift his lips again until he stopped by the bed and let her feet slide to the floor, and then it was only a moment before his mouth glued itself to hers again. She stood without struggle, aching with joy in every muscle and cell, as his hands stripped off her jacket and tossed it aside. Then her hands moved up to cling to him, and the heat of his body warmed her all through.

His hands trembled between her breasts as he opened the buttons of her shirt and then pulled that, too, down her arms. She laughed once under his kiss, from pure joy, as the cuffs locked her wrists and refused to set her free. He lifted his mouth again then, and wrestled the shirt back up her arms before bending to the task of the tiny buttons there.

Then it was the heat of his hands against her shoulders, her arms, her back, stroking and possessing until she almost melted where she stood.

"I couldn't stay away any longer," she whispered. "I'm sorry," she added foolishly, because she might as well have gone to him ages ago if she was going to give in in the end.

He pulled her hungrily in to his chest and his mouth seemed to devour hers, as if to wipe the apology from her lips.

"Don't apologize to me for needing me!" he commanded roughly.

In a few moments he had disposed of her boots and socks and jeans, and now he lifted her again and laid her down on her bed. Then as she watched, he stripped himself, with a contained fury that thrilled her.

He approached the bed, and she shivered with anticipation. He stretched out beside her, drawing the duvet up over them both, and then lay back and drew her over his chest, her hair falling down over her shoulder to touch his shoulder with an effect like an electrical connection between them.

His hands cupped her face, her hands stroked his hair, and for a moment they simply breathed and gazed into each other's eyes by the glow of lamplight.

Then he drew her head down to meet his hungry, desperate kiss. His lips and mouth and tongue pressed, demanded, took, till she was faint with the shivers of desire that raced through her, head and heart and womb.

She felt dizzy, and he was swinging up to roll her over on her back, and now lay above her. Her hair splayed out over the pillow, where he had alternately dreamed and despaired of seeing it during the long, lonely nights when he wrestled with his demons.

"I love you," he said. "I am an insane man without you."

It roared through her like a forest fire of heat and delight, and when his hands slipped under her back and found the clasp of her bra, when she saw his eyes half close as he drew the fabric away to reveal her breasts, she felt desire burn out from the deepest parts of her soul and engulf her.

She cried his name as he tenderly, passionately, stroked her breasts, kissed them, pressed the nipples between his lips in a gesture that sent heat and melting to her loins. She pulled at him, wanting completion more desperately than she had ever wanted oxygen. But he merely smiled and shook his head with a lazy look hiding a hungry determination that made her gasp almost in fear.

"This time I will take my time," he promised, and she nearly fainted just with that.

He took his time, and he was an expert, and no demons tormented him now, nor threatened his control, though he had waited for her for long hungry weeks and his body was starved for her.

He stroked her, kissed her, breasts and face and hair and throat, and always returning to her mouth, to nibble and lick and love with profoundest tenderness.

Only when she began a high panting of inexpressible need did his hands slip lower, to the edge of her briefs, and lower, to her thighs, and between her legs, where a blast of heat surged up through her to meet his touch, and her eyes went wide with surprise.

She had never experienced such hunger, and he was only distantly surprised to discover that neither had he. It burned deep inside him, a passionate intensity that he had believed himself incapable of. That he hadn't really thought anyone capable of, though men sang and wrote of it often enough. He had only half believed them.

As his hands of their own accord caught the fabric of her briefs and drew them down her legs, as he pushed her thighs apart, as he trailed kisses from her stomach down towards his destination, he felt the deep burning surge of some new capacity being born in him, and as his hands carefully lifted apart the precious folds of flesh and his mouth pressed a kiss against the tiny perfect rosebud, he felt a feeling at once wildly primitive and deeply spiritual flame up in his heart and his loins.

When she felt that touch of his warm, wet mouth, of his perfectly gentle fingers, felt how he exposed her tender centre to the flame of his need, Bel felt a cry in her own throat. Delicious, sweet, honeyed sensation rushed up her body to blacken her brain and move her to some other dimension. She felt his touch, she knew it was his tongue rasping the little knot of compacted pleasure, but in that

other, starry world it was light and heat, it was an inde-
scribable source of all she needed.

His hands cupped her buttocks, drawing her up to his
intimate kiss, reading her response as she tensed and trembled and yearned. When the stars exploded he pressed his
rasping tongue harder against her, and heard her cries of
release and gratitude with the deepest satisfaction he had
ever felt.

She lost count of the times his tongue performed that
ritual dance for her pleasure, lost count of her moans of
delight. But then at last his hands loosed her and he
loomed up over her in the bed.

"Spread your legs wide for me, Bel," he whispered,
and slipped into the cradle of her hips as she obeyed.

"It will hurt a little," he whispered, for suddenly he
knew all about virginity, though once it had terrified him.
He had taken it from her before, technically, but he knew
that in her soul she was still a virgin. The responsibility
no longer frightened him. He would look after her. He
would take care of her. Not only tonight, but as long as
he lived.

She felt him press against her, his flesh hard and urgent,
felt his hand part those tender lips again, and then slowly,
waiting as the honey of her own need came to ease his
entrance, inch by long hungry inch he pushed his way
home.

Now his passion, like a leopard on a leash, slipped its
collar and began to run in long, easy strides through the
forest of desire. He felt it could run forever.

"Ohhh!" she cried, as pain and satisfaction joined in
her and she felt the perfection of being one with her dark
lover. Then, as he drew back and pressed home again, and
again and again, each time a little less gently, each time,

little by little, letting his passion escape, the pain disappeared and pleasure began to take its place.

Now a deeper, more primitive hunger arose in her, wild, rasping, almost frightening in its intensity. She had never known before the meaning of passion, but she felt it sear through her being and leave its unmistakable mark on her. She cried aloud in a surprised mixture of hunger, yearning, need and delight as pleasure from his touch coursed through her.

"Jake!" she cried, in deep animal surprise, and then the world exploded and fell down all around her like stars, and she clung to him in the bright shimmering wreckage and felt him still pushing inside, over and over....

His beast ran and ran, muscles bunching and stretching with easy effortlessness, and pleasure shivered through him time after time, beckoning him to the feast, but he let it run on. Beneath him her face contorted with surprise and pleasure, and he felt a deep possessiveness that said she was his forever, through everything that would come.

It was then, while that thought tumbled through his mind, that the leopard shifted its pace, began to run faster and harder, and with powerful urgency Jake slipped his hand under her lower body and drew her up against him. The passion and intensity made the breath hiss between her teeth, the urgent pleasure clenched his jaw and opened his eyes to gaze hungrily at her.

The naked need in him brought another rush of pleasure flooding up in her, and Bel began to pant and press up against him, hungry for every new thing he could show her and give her.

And then the beast gathered itself tighter and tighter, and bunched to spring, and leapt...and then pleasure and joy coursed through his blood, and he cried her name aloud, as she cried his, and for the first time, love and pleasure at once possessed him.

He cried his love to her wildly as he submitted to his joy, and then, for one unrepeatable, unbelievable moment, he understood everything there was to know.

Sixteen

He drew her into her arms and held her, cupping her head against his chest, making her like something irreplaceably precious, as slowly, slowly, they both returned to the ordinary world.

"You went to my place?" he asked.

"I didn't know that's where I was headed, but that's where I ended up."

"Well I'm one up on you, then," he said. "I knew I was headed here." His voice was rough with feeling, and she trembled with happiness.

"Did you?"

"Yes, and long enough it took me to know my own mind. I told myself it was my own damned fault if you had decided…" He didn't finish. "But that didn't make it any better. I spent the worst hours of my life in your hallway, imagining you with a man, telling myself I didn't know my luck when it was in my hands."

"It's funny," she said. "I rang your doorbell, and then I suddenly just ran. I was convinced you'd already gone and found another woman, and that would have killed me."

"I'd have half killed any man fool enough to have come home with you, so I guess it amounts to the same thing."

He wrapped her tightly for a moment, saying nothing.

"It took me a long time, Bel. Too long. But I made the connection in the end."

Her heart began to pound. "What connection?" she tried to ask, in a hoarse whisper that caught in her throat. "What connection?"

He tried to put the facts of his many-petalled discovery into words. "The understanding that my life is in my own hands. That something worth having is worth taking the risk for, and the more valuable the prize, the higher and more terrifying the risk. And I've never seen it more clearly than tonight, when I had to face the fact that I might have lost you. It was all there in one."

She was afraid to speak, afraid to ask, in case he wasn't saying what he seemed to be saying. In case this was a dream and he wasn't here at all.

"I love you, Bel. I love you more than I thought it possible to love anyone or anything in this world," Jake said.

He lifted himself over her on one elbow, tenderly lifted a lock of hair from her cheek, and gazed into her eyes. "We can make it work, I know that now. All we have to do is want to do it strongly enough. Will you take the risk with me? I want you to marry me, I want to face the future with you."

The tears were already not far from the surface. They

spilled into her eyes. One flooded over and forged a trail down her cheek.

"Oh, Jake!" she cried helplessly.

His arm tightened unmercifully around her and he cried, "Bel, don't say no! I've been so stupid and blind and cowardly, but don't say I'm too late...."

He ran out of speech, though he had pleaded many urgent cases in his career, and he lowered his mouth and kissed her. He felt the loving surrender on her lips and raised his head again.

Her eyes glowed up into his. "Will you marry me, Bel?" he asked again.

"Oh, Jake, are you sure it's what you want?"

"Yes, I'm sure it's what I want," he growled. "It's what I've wanted from the first moment of setting eyes on you. Only I was too much of a coward to admit it. You called me a coward and you were right."

"Did I?" Bel asked, a little shocked.

He smiled and traced a finger around her brow and eyelid and down to the corner of her mouth. "You did, and you had every right to say it and think it. It was cowardice that made me imagine I had to accept my grandmother's reading of my life, or follow my grandfather's footsteps. I don't have to accept any of that. It was just a convenient excuse. The truth is, what I felt, and what that meant, terrified me."

"Oh," she said faintly.

"You haven't answered me," he said. "Will you marry me, and have children with me, and build your future with mine all the rest of our lives?"

The smile trembled on her lips. "Ye-es," Bel said thoughtfully. "I think I could manage that."

He made love to her again and then again, and in between they talked. He told her about his visit to his father, about how wrong his grandmother's brainwashing had been. And when she reacted indignantly, he kissed her and made love to her again.

"What day is it?" Bel asked once in faint confusion, a smile of such tender satisfaction and love in her eyes it was all he could do not to start again.

"The first day of the rest of our lives," he responded, making her laugh with delight. "Also Saturday."

"Oh. Jake, I'm so glad you changed your mind!"

"It was the only way you were ever going to allow me to make good," he joked. "A man's got his pride, you know."

She blushed and laughed, and marvelled at how different two days could be. Yesterday she had felt as if misery was etched on her soul, and today she was happier than she could have dreamed of being.

"You were so worried about that, but I wasn't. I enjoyed that night," she told him.

"A kind but unnecessary lie," Jake said with a smile.

"It's not a lie! I thought it was fabulous, only it—it…"

"Was over a little too soon," Jake supplied. "Thank you."

"That is *not* what I was going to say!"

"It doesn't matter what your opinion was, Bel, you were a virgin!" Jake pointed out inarguably. "I knew what I'd done, whatever you thought."

She was suddenly shy. "Anyway, I see the difference now, so actually you were right," she told him, in a voice that made him shout with laughter. "Why were you so horrified to learn I was a virgin, Jake?"

He was silent, collecting his thoughts. "I suppose the

truth is, because I was so shaken by it. I loved you, though I hadn't admitted it to myself. And I wouldn't have said your being a virgin had any meaning, except in that it meant I should have left you alone. But it did. It affected me to the root. So I lost control. I've never felt anything like it in my life.'' He paused and kissed her gently, like a breath across her lips. ''Until tonight.''

Later she lay gazing at him in silence. ''Jake, are you sure?''

He frowned. ''Am I sure what?'' he asked roughly.

''That this is what you want? Because if you aren't—'' She broke off.

''If I'm not—what?'' he pressed almost angrily.

She was silent.

''Come on Bel, if I'm not? You'll sleep with me for a few months and then go quietly? Is that what you're trying to say?''

''No—well, yes…I mean…''

''You mean you don't really trust me? You think I'm lying to myself, or just to you, Bel?''

''Jake,'' she pleaded.

''I am not lying to you, or myself. I love you and I am never going to love another woman with anything like what I feel for you, so what would be the point in not marrying you? I want children, and I want them to be yours, and if you are imagining that what I am doing is in any way a sacrifice, Bel, think again. The only thing I have given up is fear. That's it. Fear of myself, fear of change, fear of not knowing the future. You have made me give up fear.''

She smiled and felt it enter her soul. ''Oh, Jake, that's a lovely thing to say to any person!''

He wrapped her in his arms and there was silence again.

* * *

"Are we going to Brad and Tallia's?" Bel asked in surprise. They had gone to a resturant for brunch, and Jake said he had something to show her. Then he had driven across the bridge and along the shore road. Now, almost at that familiar gate, he was slowing the car.

"Later, maybe," Jake said. "But that's not where we are headed right now."

To her puzzlement, he turned off the road at the neighbouring house to Brad's, the one that was for sale next door. While she was stll exclaiming, he parked and opened the door.

"Are we going in?" Bel babbled.

"Yeah, let's have a look, see what you think of it," he said casually.

"See what I *think* of it? Are you—you mean—"

Jake put his fingers to her lips and led her to the front door. He produced a key from his pocket and opened it.

It was filled with light that slanted this way and through the broad windows. Empty, with pale carpets and walls, but full of memory of laughter.

"Oh, it's wonderful!" Bel exclaimed. It was no traditional design, yet everything in it seemed perfectly right, from the rough black stone fireplace to the massive wooden deck outside the window, overhanging sloping ground that was covered not with a lawn, but with natural foliage, scrub and trees and probably blackberry bushes.

"There's a tree growing up through the floor of the deck!" she exclaimed in delight, and as he opened the sliding doors, she ran out. It was all wild, like a secret garden. The whole plot was filled with native trees. Beyond the trees was the familiar view of the sea and the city and Stanley Park. It was as if a house had sprung up in the bush, not disturbing what was there more than absolute necessity dictated.

Jake pushed a button, and suddenly there was a waterfall flowing down the wall at one side of the deck, into a small pond below. Bel's heart stood still.

"Oh, Jake!" she breathed. "It's just magic, isn't it?"

"I've always figured one day sooner or later I'd live in a Johnny Winterhawk house," he said. "Would you like to live next door to your sister, Bel? It's for you to say."

She didn't know why it was this that suddenly made it all real to her. Maybe that was why they called it *real* estate. Suddenly Bel was crying—but they were soft, happy tears, where two days ago they had been hard and painful. And that realization made her cry more.

"Yes, I'd love it! And you'll be next door to Brad, too! Oh, it would be so wonderful. Jake! Wouldn't it be perfect? Oh, if you mean it, please do it right away! What if someone buys it today?"

He laughed and grabbed her in a wild hug that lifted her right off the ground, and swung her around. Then he lowered her to the ground, bent and kissed her. "I bought it last week," he said. "I was still telling myself it would make a good investment, but I know now what kind of investment I was hoping it would be. Shall we go next door and tell them the news?"

Tallia and Brad were sitting by the pool in warm terry robes when Bel and Jake drove in. Brad only raised an interested eyebrow, but Tallia looked around and leapt to her feet in delight when she saw who Jake had with him.

"Bel!" she shrieked.

"I see you took my words to heart," was all Brad said. But there was no mistaking his pleasure and approval.

"Are you—are you—tell me!" Tallia pleaded, not wanting to imagine more than was there. She clasped her hands together. "Did you just pick her up hitchhiking, or what, Jake?"

"That's about it, yeah," Jake said.

"If I'd known it was him, I'd never have climbed into the car," Bel added. "But by the time I realized, he'd taken off. Seemed easier to—"

"Tell me!" Tallia cried.

"Okay, we're an item," Bel said.

"Mmm!" Tallia said, just a little crestfallen. She had obviously been expecting more of an announcement, but was hiding her disappointment well. "Well, that's just great!"

"Come on, what's the scoop?" Brad demanded.

"Now Brad!" Tallia threw him a panicky look, but Brad only shook his head and smiled reassuringly at her.

"Well, we have news," Jake said. "In fact, we have an announcement to make."

"Oh, how *wonderful!*" shrieked Tallia. "Oh, little sister, I'm so happy!" She enveloped her sister in a hug. "I said you wouldn't, I said—but I'm so glad you did!"

"What exactly is the announcement?" Brad asked. "I mean, are we taking baseball team here?"

The girls stared at him.

"We are talking baseball team," Jake assured him solemnly.

"Great. Great," Brad said, getting to his feet.

Tallia and Bel stared at each other, then at Jake and Brad, who were shaking hands and thumping each other on the back.

"You're talking *baseball team?*" Tallia demanded in disbelief, her eyes narrowed dangerously. "*What* baseball team?"

Jake and Brad were still grinning happily. They turned to Tallia and Bel, whose amazed and infuriated faces were glaring their way. Men were terrible about emotions, but could they really possibly be talking *baseball* at a time like this?

"We are talking," Brad said softly, "about the Drummond Slingers. Or do I mean the Slinging Drummonds? Great little team. Not major league, maybe, but the hottest thing around here, for sure. And at least eight on the team."

It took them a second to get it. Then the two sisters blushed bright red. "The Drummond Slingers?" they repeated in beautiful confusion. "What are you guys talking about?"

"The future," Jake said firmly. "We're talking about the future." He looked at his coffee which had been pushed into his hand at some point. "Brad, old buddy, why do I get the feeling here that coffee is not the most appropriate drink for this occasion?"

So Brad very willingly went up to the house and came back with a couple of bottles of champagne and four glasses on a tray, and they popped the first bottle and drank to Bel and Jake's engagement.

"Wait! We have to drink to Brad and Jake's new relationship!" Tallia said. "You'll be brothers-in-law now, think of that!"

"In for a penny, in for a pound," Brad was heard to murmur.

"And one day, in the not too distant future, let's hope, we'll all be uncles and aunts!" said Jake with a grin.

"This could get complicated, in fact," Brad added, as they drank to being uncles and aunts.

Bel couldn't stand the suspense. She jumped to her feet. "There's one other new relationship we haven't told you about yet, and I sure hope, Brad and Tallia, that you'll want to drink to that!"

"What?"

"Guess!" demanded Bel, shushing Jake imperiously before he could speak.

"Well, we're already sisters, we can't get closer than that, can we?"

"Depends what you mean by close!"

"Godmothers and godfathers?"

"No, but let's drink to that!"

They drank to godmothers and godfathers.

"Baseball coach?" Brad suggested.

"I'll drink to that!"

Bel couldn't hold it in any longer. *"Neighbours!"* she cried.

Tallia's eyes grew round. Brad merely looked at Jake and nodded, as if he should have thought of this himself.

"Neighbours?" Tallia demanded. "What, what? *Tell* me!"

Bel hiccupped delicately. "My fiancé has just pur-purchased the house next door," she announced, waving her arm like a conjuror in the relevant direction and slopping champagne over her hand.

"Oh, Bel! Is it true?" Tallia breathed. She turned to Jake. "Really?"

Bel nodded firmly, if a little woozily. "Yup." She said, then gazed down at her hand. "I don't hold my champagne very well, do I?" she murmured.

"You don't, but this is not normally what we mean by

that expression, beloved," Jake said with a grin. He leaned forward, took the champagne glass out of her hand, carefully placed his lips over the champagne spills on the fleshy part of her thumb, and sucked the droplets off.

"I've been wanting to do that," he said in satisfaction.

*   *   *   *   *

*Don't miss the next highly sensual,
romantic love story in Alexandra Sellers's popular
SONS OF THE DESERT miniseries,
SHEIKH'S TEMPTATION, on sale February 2000.*

If you enjoyed what you just read,
then we've got an offer you can't resist!

Take 2 bestselling love stories FREE!

Plus get a FREE surprise gift!

**Start celebrating Silhouette's 20th anniversary
with these 4 special titles by
New York Times bestselling authors**

*Fire and Rain**
by Elizabeth Lowell

King of the Castle
by Heather Graham Pozzessere

*State Secrets**
by Linda Lael Miller

*Paint Me Rainbows**
by Fern Michaels

On sale in December 1999

Available at your favorite retail outlet
*Also available on audio from Brilliance.

Silhouette®
Where love comes alive™

Visit us at www.romance.net

PSNYT_R

Special Edition is celebrating Silhouette's 20th anniversary!

Special Edition brings you:

• brand-new LONG, TALL TEXANS
Matt Caldwell: Texas Tycoon by **Diana Palmer**
(January 2000)

• a bestselling miniseries
PRESCRIPTION: MARRIAGE
(December 1999-February 2000)
Marriage may be just what the doctor ordered!

• a brand-new miniseries SO MANY BABIES
(January-April 2000)
At the Buttonwood Baby Clinic,
lots of babies—and love—abound

• the exciting conclusion of ROYALLY WED!
(February 2000)

• the new AND BABY MAKES THREE:
THE DELACOURTS OF TEXAS
by **Sherryl Woods**
(December 1999, March & July 2000)

And on sale in June 2000, don't miss
Nora Roberts' brand-new story
Irish Rebel
in **Special Edition**.

Available at your favorite retail outlet.

Silhouette®
Where love comes alive™